"Is that meant to scare me?" Victoria asked quietly. "You do know my father's been trying to marry me off since I turned eighteen, don't you? What kind of futures do you think I've imagined for myself over the years, all far bleaker than this?"

She did not say that none of those had ever promised the faintest hint of happiness at any point. Much less passion. Maybe that was a good thing. Maybe she would have been better off with a man who had sex with her only to produce children, then swanned off to his preferred bits on the side and left her to it.

That had always sounded like the best of all possible conclusions to her father's obsession.

"I'm not afraid of our future, Ago. I'm just pleased that I'm no longer in my father's prison. That's enough."

But he did not smile back at her.

He did not smile at all. "You may well find your circumstances more prison-like than you anticipated, Victoria. Because I will have no scandal attached to my heir." He nodded, as if that was the end of the discussion. "No matter what."

The Outrageous Accardi Brothers

A marriage deal with two happily-ever-afters...

The two brothers running the notorious Accardi Corporation are total opposites but have the same goal: elevate the Accardi empire.

Known for his playboy antics, wild card Tiziano Accardi has one final chance to prove to his elder brother, Ago, that he's more than his extracurricular activities through a very convenient marriage. But when he makes the most unexpected of choices, both brothers' worlds will be flipped upside down!

Tiziano must marry the innocent Cameron heiress or lose his position in the Accardi Corporation, but he has other plans. And when he bumps into Annie, she becomes the perfect solution to all of his problems...

Read Tiziano and Annie's story in
The Christmas He Claimed the Secretary

After a lifetime of clearing up his brother's messes, apologizing to Victoria Cameron is the least Ago can do. Only he never expected that *they* would share one night or that it would have forever consequences!

Read Ago and Victoria's story in
The Accidental Accardi Heir

Both available now!

Caitlin Crews

THE ACCIDENTAL ACCARDI HEIR

HARLEQUIN
PRESENTS

Recycling programs for this product may not exist in your area.

ISBN-13: 978-1-335-73895-0

The Accidental Accardi Heir

For questions and comments about the quality of this book, please contact us at CustomerService@Harlequin.com.

Harlequin Enterprises ULC
22 Adelaide St. West, 41st Floor
Toronto, Ontario M5H 4E3, Canada
www.Harlequin.com

Printed in U.S.A.

USA TODAY bestselling, RITA® Award–nominated and critically acclaimed author **Caitlin Crews** has written more than one hundred books and counting. She has a master's and PhD in English literature, thinks everyone should read more category romance and is always available to discuss her beloved alpha heroes. Just ask. She lives in the Pacific Northwest with her comic book artist husband, is always planning her next trip and will never, ever, read all the books in her to-be-read pile. Thank goodness.

Books by Caitlin Crews

Harlequin Presents

The Sicilian's Forgotten Wife
The Bride He Stole for Christmas
Willed to Wed Him

The Outrageous Accardi Brothers

The Christmas He Claimed the Secretary

Pregnant Princesses

The Scandal That Made Her His Queen

The Lost Princess Scandal

Crowning His Lost Princess
Reclaiming His Ruined Princess

Visit the Author Profile page
at Harlequin.com for more titles.

CHAPTER ONE

THE LAST PERSON Ago Accardi ever wanted to see again was Victoria Cameron.

Particularly not clad in a simple white gown, clutching a bouquet of flowers, and walking down the aisle of the ancient chapel on his family's ancient estate in the rolling hills of Tuscany.

Heading for the groom standing at the altar, however reluctantly.

That groom being—quite literally for his sins—Ago himself.

He clenched his teeth as she approached in a serene fashion that he could only call insulting, given the circumstances of this wedding. He was somewhat shocked that his jaw did not shatter at the impact.

For this was not at all how Ago Accardi, known far and wide for his commitment to his duty, his uncompromising commitment to his responsibilities, and his upright moral code, had intended to take a bride.

While no one was holding an actual shotgun, here in this lovely stone chapel his ancestors had built during the Renaissance, the threat remained all the same. Because there was only one reason this ceremony was taking place at all.

His gaze moved over Victoria's admittedly lovely face—damn the woman. The dress she wore was simple, but then, she needed no adornment. By any measure, she was a beautiful woman. Tall like a willow and with golden hair she wore pulled back today, so the cheerful innocence she wore was visible to all and took the place of any intricate veil or dramatic lace.

But then he dropped his eyes to the unmistakably round and high and obviously pregnant belly that preceded her up the short aisle, making a mockery of her innocent expression.

That belly that had altered the course of his meticulously plotted and carefully constructed life.

That belly was the reason this wedding was taking place in a secluded chapel, hidden away on the grounds of the vast Accardi estate, rather than in the cathedral Ago's consequence, wealth, and aristocratic lineage would normally have demanded. To say nothing of hers.

She and her belly and her irate father had been presented to him a mere fortnight before.

They had paraded into his London offices as if they wanted all the world to see that the belly attached to the famously virginal Victoria Cameron, daughter of one of Accardi Industries' best clients, was *inarguably* that of a pregnant woman.

And, therefore, their presence in the Accardi Industries headquarters could only mean one thing.

For a year ago, Victoria had been engaged—well, *nearly* engaged, to be precise—to Ago's younger brother, who had not had the slightest intention of marrying her despite knowing it was Ago's wish that he do so. This was something Ago had intended to ignore, because to his way of thinking it was high time that the famously disgraceful Tiziano settle down. That he actually did something for the family, did his part, did more—in other words—than simply tomcat about the globe, notching bedposts everywhere he roamed.

Ago should have known that his little brother could not be told a thing.

For instead of following directions, Tiziano had chosen to fall dramatically and publicly in love. With a woman Ago would never have chosen for him.

Not least because the woman in question had been, before her relationship with Tiziano—or so Ago chose to believe, having decided not to question his brother's timing too closely—a secretary. At Accardi Industries.

The entire thing had been a nightmare, because Ago had gone to the trouble not only of insisting that Tiziano married, but of picking out Victoria Cameron and arranging the match with her father. As if it was still the Renaissance.

And he already knew the whispers. His brother had called him last week, laughing at the tabloid reports that Everard Cameron's daughter—the paragon of virtue who was too saintly to succumb to temptation, according to Tiziano—had gone and turned up pregnant.

Proving herself as unholy as anyone else.

They are certain to think it's mine, Tiziano had said with a great big laugh.

Ago had not laughed.

He was not laughing now.

Especially as Victoria drew closer.

Her father stood like a thundercloud in the nearest pew, watching Ago like a hawk, as if Ago was likely to make a break for it. Ago's side was empty. Who should he invite, he had asked himself, with all attendant scorn? Who did he wish to take part in this demonstration of his own distasteful fallibility and irredeemable disgrace?

It was bad enough that it was happening. Ago saw no reason why he should compound the issue by issuing invitations to his own sordid downfall.

That choice had made the past several days markedly unpleasant. For Everard Cameron was the kind of man who never vented his spleen once when he could do so consistently, and with increasing venom each time.

When he had first marched his daughter into Ago's office, he, as Tiziano no doubt would have suspected, had not suspected Ago himself of any perfidy.

Indeed, who would dare?

Look at the state of my daughter! Everard had thundered. *Look at what your unsavory cretin of a brother has done!*

Ago had looked. Victoria was tall and slender, an immaculate golden blonde who radiated a serene and implacable contentment—no matter what she might or might not have been feeling inside. As he knew to his cost. The fact that she'd sported that obvious belly that she had not possessed the last time he'd seen her had in no way been concealed by the dress she wore. She had stood there in his office, her hands propped up on the belly in question and her eyes demurely lowered to the floor.

He had felt his pulse beat in the hinge of his clenched jaw, hard. Then harder still.

My brother is quite famously besotted, Ago had replied, faintly surprised that he'd been able to push words out at all.

As if that matters for a wastrel like him! Everard Cameron had cried.

Has Victoria indicated that Tiziano got her in this state? Ago had asked, his voice an icy scrape across the length of his office, as if he, personally was ushering in a winter of snowstorms and icicles with his words alone. As if he possessed such magic.

Everard did not glance at his daughter. He never did, Ago had noticed. To him, Victoria was nothing but a pawn in the game the older man had been playing his whole life—that being, how to gather as much wealth as possible before he died. And knowing him, find a way to take it with him when he quit this mortal coil.

Needless to say, an unplanned pregnancy did not permit Everard to hawk his daughter's virtue in the way he was accustomed to doing. The way he had been doing all this time. Having jealously guarded her virginity, surrounding her with guards after she graduated from a long series of dreary convent schools, he had presented her to the wealthy men of his acquaintance as the perfect broodmare.

For a hefty price.

And for a certain kind of man, who was focused on his dynasty above all else, Victoria Cameron was a prize indeed.

A prize that Tiziano had long said Ago should

claim for himself, more than once, since he appeared so enamored by her.

But Ago had been focused on sorting out his brother's notoriety, not his own dynastic requirements. Because *he* was Ago Accardi, blameless and beyond reproach. He had been toying with the dossiers of no less than five different spotless heiresses at this time last year and confidently expected that any one of them would leap at the chance to become the next Accardi matriarch.

He had intended that he should marry only once the Tiziano problem was solved, and he had been making good on that intention now that Tiziano had made it clear he would never part from his mistress. And, indeed, intended to marry her.

Which was, Ago supposed, better than never intending to marry at all.

But the perfect bloodlines the Accardi legacy required were down to him, as ever. Thus, in this past year, Ago had painstakingly narrowed his list of selections down to only two remaining spotless young things, each of them overawed by him.

To an exasperating degree, he could admit.

Only now, here, where their fawning and fidgeting was no longer something he need concern himself with.

Victoria Cameron, who too many were aware had been intended for Tiziano and then summarily jilted by him—the scandalous tabloid articles all but wrote themselves and Ago made it a point to never, ever feed the tabloids—had never been on his list.

Yet here they were.

The only thing my daughter has said in her defense, Everard Cameron had growled a fortnight ago, *was* Accardi Industries. *You and I both know what that must mean.*

It was clear that the man meant Tiziano and his well-known whoring about.

And it had only been then, as her father's implication hung thick in the air, that Victoria had finally raised her clear blue gaze from the floor. Just enough to meet Ago's for a swift instant, then fall again.

But he had seen all he needed to see.

And worse still, he had—once again—found himself in a crisis of temptation thanks to this woman.

It was unendurable.

Six months ago, Ago had been confronted by that temptation, and he had failed. In every possible way.

And a fortnight ago, he had understood that she was giving him a way out. Ago could blame his brother. It would be easy, especially as Cameron already assumed Tiziano was the one to blame. Ago could neatly sidestep his responsibility where she was concerned and blame the man that most would assume had gotten her with child anyway.

But somehow, looking at her rounded belly and knowing precisely how she had come to find herself in that condition, Ago had not been able to do it.

He had not been able to force the words to his tongue.

Even attempting to do so had made him feel something like ill.

He had willed her silently to look at him again, but she did not. Because Victoria Cameron was many things, as he had discovered that night six months ago, but *overawed* was not one of them.

So instead, Ago had looked at her father.

Your daughter and I will be wed as quickly as possible, he had said coldly.

Then he'd strode from the room to order his staff to make the arrangements—and to put off having to field Everard Cameron's outraged sputtering.

And in those two weeks, he had not found himself alone with his soon-to-be bride. He had made certain he was never left on his own in her presence, in fact, as no good could possibly come of that.

No good had already come of it.

Her father, on the other hand, could only be put off so long. There had been great deal of yelling, in two countries so far. Ago had been obliged to put in an appearance at the older man's stately pile in Wiltshire on no less than three separate occasions. He had been half hoping that Cameron would come to his senses and remember that this was not, in fact, medieval times. Maybe then he would simply…not turn up on the celebrated Accardi lands, sprawling across numerous acres in the idyllic Tuscan countryside.

Though even if that had occurred, Ago knew himself well enough to know that he was not the sort of man who was all that interested in the trappings of modernity. Medieval Italy lived in his blood, his bones.

And the fact of the matter was that Victoria Cameron was carrying his heir.

As such, no matter what her father did or did not do, there had only ever been one solution.

Something he'd repeated to her father only last night as the older man had seethed and shouted down his study in the stately old villa, demanding more concessions from Ago.

As a matter of honor, Ago had told him, standing with his back to the room so Cameron could not see how truly finished with this discussion he was, *I am refusing any gesture toward a dowry, Everard. But do not presume to press my goodwill any further. I do not think you will like where we end up.*

Here in the chapel, Ago caught the eye of the

priest—who was some or other Accardi cousin, according to local lore. Then he returned his gaze to Victoria, who was gliding to a stop before him.

Ago did not know if her father had not walked her down the aisle because he was punishing her in some way, or if she had refused his arm. If he had to guess, he would suspect the latter. For he knew better than most, did he not, that Victoria Cameron was not at all as under her father's control as he might imagine she was.

Something in him seemed to thunder, and rage, though he knew well not a hint of it appeared on his face. That same storm and clamor roared as he took her hand. He held it as he nodded curtly to her father, seething in his pew, and then turned to the priest before them.

Victoria's hand gripped his, tight, and that did not help matters any. It made that storm in him grow teeth, even as it howled all the louder. He wanted to drop her hand as if it was on fire. He wanted to toss it aside—

And then somehow turn back time and prevent himself from ever holding onto her in the first place.

But Ago had been a man of duty his whole life. He might not like what this woman represented. He might resent, with every particle of his being, that she had proven to him, in no uncertain terms, that he was nothing more than a man. And an unworthy man, at that.

Yet that did not mean he was not prepared to do his duty.

He thought of his own difficult father as the family priest began the ceremony, and he repeated the age-old words when necessary. He thought of his grandfather, even more uncompromisingly stern in his day, as Victoria sweetly repeated her own words back.

Ago knew well that both his father and grandfather would despair of the choices he had made, and the dishonor he had brought upon the family name—and yet both would applaud, in the end, that Ago was facing up to his actions and responsibilities so squarely.

Especially because Victoria was carrying his child.

The next Accardi heir.

All potential scandal and personal disgrace aside, that was the only thing that truly mattered, as both his father and grandfather had impressed upon him. At length. It was Ago's responsibility to make certain that the Accardi legacy continued well into the future. And more, that his own son followed in his footsteps, not his brother's— living a life of service to his august name when it was his turn.

As Ago himself had always done, before Victoria.

He told himself that this was what fueled him as the priest waved his hands over Ago and Victoria at last, pronouncing them man and wife.

Ago leaned closer, pressing an impatient kiss on his new bride's mouth. It was swift. Peremptory at best. He told himself he was imagining the wave of heat within him.

Once it was done he turned abruptly, ushering her toward the chapel door whether she wished to go or not.

Though she did not resist. Instead, she matched her long-legged stride to his, moving swiftly with him in a kind of concert he chose not to focus on too closely. For reasons he did not intend to dig into.

Once outside, he marched her halfway down the lane of stately cypress trees that led back to the main house before he remembered it was not necessary for him to keep holding her hand.

He dropped it.

As if it really was on fire.

"That's that, then, isn't it?" Victoria said, rather too brightly. With what sounded like laughter in her voice, when this was obviously no occasion for levity of any kind. "We're married."

And then, to his astonishment, she actually *let out* a laugh. As if she couldn't quite believe it. As if something magical and wondrous had occurred here today.

Ago looked back toward the chapel and saw that Everard had been caught up by the priest on the front step. The two looked to be deep in conversation.

No doubt debating the state of Ago's immortal soul. Or lack thereof.

But Ago took advantage of this moment. The first time he'd been alone with Victoria since that fateful night six months back.

"Is this what you had planned all along?" he demanded, his words like bullets, and for once he did not concern himself with how they might land. "Were you planning it six months ago? Was it a trap from the very start?"

He expected her denial. Perhaps some tears.

But instead, Victoria Cameron—*Victoria Accardi*, now, he corrected himself with no little bleakness and fury—fixed him with a solemn stare.

"Yes," she said, without blinking. "And no."

He glared down at her, and even though his temper was a black thing that wrapped him up tight, he was not immune to the sheer perfection of her form. The blue of her eyes, a far lighter shade than his. Her spun gold hair, pulled back at the crown and then left to flow down around her shoulders. The fine, aristocratic line of her nose. Her elegant mouth that could be, as he knew to his cost, deliciously wicked.

And he could not tell if he had always found her this tempting, even when he thought that his own brother ought to marry her. Or if this was a more recent affliction.

"I suppose I should be grateful that you actually dare admit it to my face." Ago did not feel grateful and he doubted very much that he sounded it.

Victoria, unlike his trembling heiress selections, did not look even remotely undone by his tone or likely fierce expression.

"It never occurred to me that you would look twice at me," she replied matter-of-factly. "So in that sense, there was no plan. I also never expected to run into you at that party. Even if I could have imagined that I wouldn't have assumed that you would wish to talk to me as much as you did. So again, I had no plans on that score."

It was a sunny November day in Tuscany today, though cool. And still it was far warmer than the fragile British day at the end of May when he'd run into her in a grand old home on the southern coast to do a bit of business.

He had not expected to find Victoria there. Or, having found her, that she should also be wholly unsupervised, when he had never encountered her previously without a phalanx of chaperones. But the house belonged to her father's brother, and was considered safe for his daughter's virtue. Her usual guards had not been watching her as closely as they normally did.

So it was that he had been able to walk with her in the garden on that not-quite-warm evening. Worse, he had been able to offer his apologies for what had occurred between her and his brother—or hadn't, rather—the previous Christmas.

He had not expected to find her fascinating.

And Ago was not a man who found much in this life *unexpected*.

He didn't much like that she'd managed to surprise him again now.

"You said *yes* first," he growled at her.

Victoria lifted a shoulder, then dropped it, and he could not help but notice that the look on her face was wholly unrepentant. If anything, she looked…smug?

"I couldn't have planned any of that," she reassured him. He remained wholly un-reassured. "But once it happened, I'll admit, I was hoping it would turn out like this."

"Because it is every girl's dream, is it not?" His voice was low, a silken fury, and it took more self-control than it should have to keep from wrapping his hands around her shoulders and hauling her toward him. To emphasize his outrage, he assured himself. "A shotgun wedding in a mad rush to legitimize a child before its appearance."

"My father didn't actually have a shotgun,"

Victoria said with another laugh that made that storm in him rage anew. Her gaze moved over his face, and, somehow, she laughed yet again at whatever she saw there. When he knew oligarchs and heiresses alike who would cower at the sight. "I'm sorry if this wasn't what you wanted."

"How can you doubt it?"

"I'm finally free, Ago. So if you must hate me, I accept that." Victoria shrugged again, as if to suggest the impossible. That his wishes did not matter. That he could hate her and she would not care at all. "It's a reasonable consequence."

CHAPTER TWO

Victoria was not as heedless of her brand-new husband's feelings as she might like to pretend.

Because Ago Accardi was the most darkly beautiful man she had ever encountered in her life. More than that, he was the only man she had ever so much as kissed. And things had gone great deal further than kissing, that night in her uncle Edward's garden. Sometimes, even now, the only thing she could think of was the possessive way his mouth had moved over hers. And the magic he'd taught her was in her own body, the body that he had so easily made his.

She thought about Ago entirely too much. There was no pretending otherwise on that score.

But today, at last, she was free.

Twenty-four years old and finally—*finally*—free.

And despite how masterful and overwhelming Ago seemed to her, with that brooding fury his stern face—to say nothing of the way he'd stamped that hard kiss upon her lips—the fact that she had finally escaped her father's grasp was the only thing she could concentrate on.

Especially when Everard shook off the priest, then charged down the narrow little lane to catch up to her and Ago.

It was a bright day, but cold. She could feel every single goose bump that rose on her skin, and didn't much care if it was the crisp air that reminded her it was nearly December, or the glowering man beside her. Because she felt wholly alive, at last.

Because she was *free*.

And over her dead body would the child she carried ever find itself locked up in a cage the way she'd been all this time. It didn't matter how pretty it was. A cage was a cage.

She was sure that Ago would agree. One hand moved over her belly and stayed there, protectively. Ago had to agree.

After all, he hadn't bought her for breeding purposes like all the other men her father had let sniff around her would have done, if they could have met his price. What had happened between them in that garden had been organic and unexpected.

Or he wouldn't have been so...*undone* afterward.

This time, she knew the goose bumps were thanks to her memories, not the chilly breeze.

"I hope you're happy," her father seethed at her when he caught up to them. He didn't spare a glance for Ago—but then, he'd been thundering at Ago every chance he got, for the past two weeks. Victoria wasn't too proud to listen at doors. "After all the work I put into you. After everything I gave you. This squalid ceremony is the thanks I get for all I did."

"You mean, when you raised me?" she asked mildly. "After my mother died? As was your responsibility, as my only remaining parent? Was that what you did for me, Papa?"

"To be married like this," he continued in the same tone of aggrieved outrage, because he wasn't listening to her.

Victoria wasn't sure that he had ever listened to her. As long as she kept the same serene and vaguely cheerful look on her face, she could say just about anything to him and he wouldn't register it. That was what she was to him—a bit of white noise.

"The shame," Everard intoned. "And the temerity to wear a white dress over your obviously pregnant belly. I'm glad your mother isn't alive to see the depths to which you've sunk, Victoria."

Victoria winced at that, though it was nothing new. And tame, really.

Her father had shouted far worse when her condition had become impossible to hide. Some women, she knew—because she had read half the internet in a panic—managed to keep their pregnancies hidden to the day they gave birth. But then, most women probably didn't have to contend with the kind of scrutiny her father had kept her under since she was small.

She opened her mouth to do what she always did, and deflect her father's actual hurtful words away from her.

But beside her, Ago stiffened. "Have a care, Everard," he said, in that wintry voice of his that haunted her, silk and steel. "You are speaking to my wife."

It occurred to Victoria then that rather than this being a simple matter of freeing herself from her father's clutches, she had instead turned her life into more of a frying pan to fire scenario. Yet she was going to have to wait to succumb to anxiety over that, because right now, having anyone at all speak to her father like that was…

Well, it was delightful. *A lovely wedding gift*, Victoria told herself.

Even if Ago turned out to be an ogre, at least she would have this.

"I'll talk to my daughter any way I like," her father retorted, scowling at Ago as if he could scare him off with the beetling of his brows.

"But she is no longer merely your daughter, is she?" asked Ago, with that implacable, unyielding iron that had always made him seem, to her, like so much more than merely a man. And today made her consider him nothing less than heroic. "She is wife to the current Accardi heir, and mother to the next. Victoria Cameron is no more. May I present to you, Everard, *La Signora* Victoria Accardi."

Ago said her name as if she was a stranger. He said it not just with his usual Italian-inflected English, lyrical and poetic, but as if she herself was Italian. As if he had made her so, today. He even glossed over the *c* in Victoria, as if her name was *Vittoria*.

As if she had disappeared in him as surely today as she had ever disappeared beneath her father's too-tight grip.

Victoria felt something very much like panic begin to beat at her.

Suddenly, she could remember all those little details she'd tried her best to set aside over the past six months. Not just from that night in the garden, but from all the previous times she'd interacted with the fiercely proper Ago, who seemed to wear his civility like a bit of bespoke fabric, stretched across the brutal ferocity that so defined him.

He was considered a refined, elegant gentleman. But in the same breath, the people who called him such a thing would turn around and whisper of his prowess in business, and the razor-sharp intelligence that made him the kind of weapon other men admired, feared, and wished to test themselves against in equal measure.

And more, Ago had no greater fan than her father—at least until the past two weeks, when Everard's whole world had been rocked by the astonishing knowledge that the only man he'd trusted around his daughter was the one who had defiled her.

Victoria knew better than to say such a thing to her father, much less to Ago himself, but she did not feel defiled in the least.

She was sure that would be considered bad form. Or possibly sinful. Not that she supposed it mattered now. They were married. The child would be legitimate. All the patriarchal considerations had been met and now, she dearly hoped, she would get to live the rest of her life without all the scrutiny that had marked her first twenty-four years.

Are you well? Ago had asked her when she and her father had arrived in Italy several days ago. They had been standing in one of the grand salons that seem to flow this way and that in the great house she knew full well had been in his family for more generations than her father's family had even been considered elevated from common stock.

Very well, she'd replied. For what could she say? That some weeks after that night in the garden, she'd felt under the weather—but who didn't feel that way as summer burned too hot. Then came to a close when England's fall rain took over. She'd assumed she was simply a bit gloomier than usual, that was all.

She hadn't connected that night in the garden with anything that came after. And it had been a good four months before it had occurred to her that she couldn't remember the last time she'd bled. And that, for the first time in her life, there was the possibility that such random fluctuations could mean something.

Victoria prided herself on her own intelligence, thank you, as it was all she'd had for years. And that intelligence had made it clear to her that there was no point telling Ago any of the things that had happened, particularly not before the wedding, because the wedding was her ticket out from under her father's thumb and bonus, she wasn't actively repulsed by her groom.

But also, for longer there than she cared to admit, she'd been little more than a pregnant girl afraid of what that pregnancy would mean.

More to the point, how her father would react.

And no matter how many times she'd told herself that feeling such things gave her kinship, through time, with too many other girls just like her to count, it didn't make her feel any better.

How could she tell a man as powerful as Ago such a thing? He had no idea what it was like to feel either helpless or alone. How could he?

No...complications? he had asked, as if he was inquiring after the weather.

As if he wasn't personally responsible for getting her pregnant in the first place. And as if she didn't know exactly how he'd gone about it. What it was like to have all that heat and hard steel of him wedged between her legs, thrusting in and out, setting her alive and alight at once.

No, no complications at all, she had replied smoothly, shoving the unhelpful memories aside.

It hadn't occurred to her until now that the primary complication in all of this was him.

Ago took her arm, and not in the sort of way that made her think it was wise to pull it back. Then he began to walk, at a brisk enough pace that her father was forced to break into a trot as he followed. Victoria felt cold, suddenly. The late November day had suddenly come over all British, casting aside the Tuscan sunshine, growing thin and pale.

The chapel was only a short walk from the main house, and Victoria tried her best to compose herself. She lectured herself with every step, because her uneasiness helped no one. Not her baby. Not herself.

It would give her father pleasure, and Ago too much control.

Surely she knew better.

Once inside the main house, Ago led them to a private dining room that she knew was separate from the main dining hall that could seat a battalion. His staff had prepared a small feast and he escorted her with excruciating courtesy to her seat at the bottom of the table. Then took his place at the top, waving her father in between them.

And as Victoria sat there, feeling the opposite of hungry, Ago proceeded to have one of the most boring conversations she'd ever heard with her father. As if all he could think of to discuss today were stock markets the world over.

She blew out a breath, smoothing her hands over the roundness of her belly to find her baby's head. Then she moved it around until she felt a few kicks. That made her smile, and she reminded herself that whatever happened, she'd gotten everything she wanted today. She was free of her father. There had been too many times over the past few years, as Everard took her on a tour of all the eligible men who even remotely met his standards, that she'd imagined she would end up in far worse straits than these.

Ago was no monster. He was known far and wide as a fair man, if cold.

As far as she was concerned, that was an upgrade.

Better yet, she was not alone. In a few short months, her child would be with her and she would be a mother. She could barely remember her own mother, but the little scraps of memory she still held on to involved a feeling of intense well-being, a wide smile, and love. She might not have planned to become a mother quite so soon, much less with a strange man, but now that it was happening, she had to admit that it truly was the best possible outcome she could have imagined.

And she must have lost herself in these ruminations, imagining herself cradling a tiny child in her arms, a little boy or girl with eyes as blue as hers, and hair as dark as Ago's. Because when she looked up, her father had left the room and it was only Ago and her sitting at either end of this table. A table she'd found overly large and long when they sat down at it, so formally, but now seemed entirely too small.

"Where did my father go?" she asked, because she was well trained to always, always know where her warden was. It was just common sense.

"Our discussion of the stock market led him to

make an urgent call to his investment manager," Ago said. Very coolly.

He sat back in his chair, and the gaze he leveled on her made her feel as if she should sit up straighter. As if she should retreat into that shroud of scrupulously exquisite manners that she'd learned from the nuns was nothing short of battle armor. But something in her made her stop, because she didn't want him to see her do such a thing. She wanted—desperately—to pretend that he wasn't getting to her.

"He's quite close with his investment manager," she said, with a great studied casualness. "I think he likes no one better in all the world."

Ago only eyed her for a long moment. So long that she found herself sitting up straighter despite what he might or might not see.

"This is the first time we have been alone," Ago said quietly, but not very softly. "Do you have nothing to say for yourself?"

"*La Signora Victoria Accardi* sounds like a stranger," she heard herself say, though she'd no intention of saying anything. His dark brows rose, and he gazed at her as if he failed to understand the actual words she used. It made her absurdly nervous. "I never said I would take your name."

His mouth curved, though she was not foolish

enough to think it a smile. "You carry my child and so too shall carry my name. There will be no debate on this."

Victoria had never given the issue of taking or not taking a husband's name much thought. Or any thought. But the way he said that, with such matter-of-fact arrogance, put her back up at once.

"You do know that these days, a woman gets to decide what name she takes, don't you?"

Ago did something that was not quite a shrug for he was nothing so indecisive, but still. She felt dismissed as she was clearly meant to.

"If you wish to have these debates, *mia mogliettina*, you should have married a different man." Her mouth dropped open, and something she couldn't name gleamed in his unusually dark blue eyes, but he didn't give her a chance to speak. "But unfortunately for you, you have married me. And when it comes to my work, I'm a very modern man. I value women and you need not take my word for it. It is reflected at the highest levels in my company."

"I congratulate you on doing the very barest minimum, Ago," she murmured. "How nice that you take part in the current century."

His dark eyes gleamed brighter. "But that doesn't mean that I expect the same arrangements at home. I am an Accardi. The child you carry is an Accardi. And the Accardi name is sacred to me. The Accardi legacy is the guiding force of my existence. I do not require you to understand this. To be honest, I care little if you do or not."

And now there was no mistaking that the gleaming thing in his gaze was, if nothing else, a weapon. Sharp and hot, it pinned her back against her chair.

"You may be free of your father this day. But you will never be free again, Victoria. You will be an Accardi until the day you die, and when you do, you will be interred in the family mausoleum—forever at my side. There will be no escape, ever, for either of us. I hope that this is what you wanted in that garden. I hope you are adequately prepared for the lifetime you see stretching out before you now, from this day forward."

Victoria's heart was beating much too quickly, but she made herself breathe. "And what of happiness on the way to the mausoleum?" she dared ask. "Where does that factor in?"

Ago only stared at her. "Happiness, Victoria, is for lesser men who do not have centuries of duty and tradition to occupy them."

Her throat went dry. Still, she fought to keep her reactions to herself. It was safer that way.

"Is that meant to scare me?" she asked quietly.

"You do know my father's been trying to marry me off since I turned eighteen, don't you? What kind of futures do you think I've imagined for myself over the years, all far bleaker than this?"

She did not say that none of those had ever promised the faintest hint of happiness at any point. Much less passion. Maybe that wasn't a good thing. Maybe she would have been better off with a man who had sex with her only to produce children, then swanned off to his preferred bits on the side and left her to it.

That had always sounded like the best of all possible conclusions to her father's obsession.

"Anyway," she managed to say, because she found she wasn't as sanguine about that option as she might have been once. As she'd used to be, she was certain, though it was difficult to recall a time before Ago Accardi had taken over the bulk of her daydreams. Or a time when she hadn't known what sex was like, and what might be asked of her from men she didn't find even remotely attractive in the sort of marriage her father had planned for her. "I'm not afraid of our future, Ago. I'm just pleased that I'm no longer in my father's prison. That's enough."

But he did not smile back at her.

He did not smile at all. "You may well find your circumstances more prison-like than you anticipated, Victoria. Because I will have no scandal attached to my heir." He nodded, as if that was the end of the discussion. "No matter what."

CHAPTER THREE

THE PANIC THAT had been creeping around inside her until now, mostly contained in the wild beating of her heart against her ribs, exploded.

It took everything Victoria had, every little scrap of will, and maybe the way the baby kicked inside her, to remain still. Despite all the shrapnel that seemed to batter her again and again, tearing her up inside. Despite the detonation inside her that she was terribly afraid might have melted all of her bones where she sat.

But she didn't move. She didn't blink.

Victoria was suddenly, fiercely, glad that she'd spent the whole of her life in the particular jail cell of her father's control.

It was because of all that practice that she was able to keep her reaction to herself. It was only because she'd spent years perfecting it that she was able to maintain a serene sort of smile, and no particular indication of her feelings on her face.

"'Prison-like'?" she echoed, but kept her voice free of all but the mildest curiosity. The sort she might employ if making an inquiry about train timetables or some other such tedious thing. She wasn't sure she had ever been more proud of herself. "That sounds unduly aggressive, surely."

"While your father has been entertaining himself by upbraiding me at every opportunity," Ago continued in that low, cold voice of his, clearly unaware that she had blown up, right there in front of him, "I have been considering the situation we find ourselves in."

She was frozen solid, stuck in her seat. Victoria didn't think she could have risen to her feet if her life depended on it, and so she did not try. She stayed where she was, furiously trying to make herself over into a study of polite indifference.

"Have you indeed?" she asked. "Personally, I always recite old poetry in my head while he lectures me. *'My father moved through dooms of love,'* and so on. As you do."

"I'm not a man of passion, Victoria." Ago's voice was little more than a growl. Maybe that was why the way he said her name seemed to settle deep inside her, like some kind of deep foundation. And again, there was that glittering thing in his gaze that felt like another detonation. "Despite the impression you may have of me."

She knew she should say something. Something witty and amusing to pop the tension in the room. The tension thrumming inside her. But somehow, Victoria couldn't seem to speak. It was as if his hand gripped her throat, though he sat down the length of the table. It was as if he was preventing her from saying even one of the words that crowded there on her tongue, too tangled up was she in stormy dark blue *glittering* and her sudden inability to think of anything but Ago Accardi and *passion*…

"I'm a careful man," he told her. "Unlike my brother, who has done as he pleased since infancy, my life has always been an expression of my duty. I have always thought first and foremost of my responsibilities, for I owe nothing less to both those who came before me, and those who will come after."

He inclined his head at her rounded belly as if he was anointing his heir then and there, and Victoria stiffened. She found herself folding her hands over her belly and coming *this close* to frowning at him straight out.

Because she did not want him turning *her child* into…whatever he was, so grim and humorless, thank you.

"Your brother never seemed the least bit unaware of the fact he was an Accardi," she pointed out, though she was not the authority on Tiziano Accardi, by any means. Despite having been very nearly married off to him, she thought she'd only spoken to him about four times in her life.

Still, the younger Accardi brother left a lasting impression. She'd concluded long ago that it was only *because* he was an Accardi that he was always so over-the-top—though even he had settled down now that he'd found the right woman. The right woman who was, thankfully, not her.

"I love my brother," Ago replied, dark and gruff. "He is the only family I have left, so I do not begrudge him the happiness he appears to have discovered in so unlikely a place. But his commitment to playing the role of the world's greatest cad did nothing but cause me difficulties. The more outrageous his behavior, the more scrupulously correct mine has always been. And yet there are already whispers about you, Victoria. There will be those who will never believe that your child is not Tiziano's. And this, you see, I cannot allow."

She still felt that phantom hand at her throat, and tighter now. And for some reason, her eyes seemed determined to tear up.

"People will always whisper," she managed to say. "It has nothing to do with what you will or will not allow. Even you, Ago, cannot control the world's favorite pastime. They will all gossip merrily no matter what you do."

"Perhaps," he said, but not as if he truly believed that he, Ago Accardi, could not bend the world to his will if he chose.

He pushed back from the table then, and stood. And the way he stood...affected her.

A new kind of detonation rolled out inside her, but this one was all heat and flame.

It was as if Victoria had somehow been so focused on what her wedding would bring her, personally, that she'd...overlooked the groom.

Not that there was any *overlooking* Ago.

But for some reason, now that he was standing there before her and they were alone—and *married*—the only thing she could focus on was how straight and tall and relentlessly *masculine* he was. How his body was a symphony of lean muscle, somehow filling out his dark, bespoke suit with an edgy ferocity that only looked smooth and sophisticated from a distance. Up close, or contained in a small dining room, he seemed to be made entirely of sparks. They made the very air she breathed sizzle as she inhaled.

And as he looked at her with those eyes that should not have been dark blue, not with all that dark brown hair, the sizzle only deepened until it felt a great deal like an open flame.

"Mia mogliettina," he said, very distinctly, and while she didn't know exactly what he meant by that, calling her *mia mogliettina*, it was clear the words were not any kind of endearment, "I do not

have to control the world. I need only control my life. And now that we are wed, that means you. My little wife."

Again, she felt that choking sensation, but this time it seemed to link up with all of those sparks, shifting straight over into the kind of crackling, dancing flames she associated with that night in her uncle's garden. The night she tried her best not to think about, because it was all too…hot and intense and outside the bounds of everything her existence had ever been, before and after.

Victoria wanted to leap to her own feet, possibly even run from the room, but all she could seem to do was stare at him.

In horror, she told herself primly. *You are flushed straight through with* horror *at the thought of Ago Accardi's* control.

Though that was not how she would describe the way he'd held her in that garden and—

Focus, she ordered herself, with no small amount of disgust at her own susceptibility, then and now. *He's talking about imprisonment, not passion.*

"You will stay here," he was saying, sounding and looking matter-of-fact, at best. As if he was delivering some kind of corporate status report instead of the terms of her new life sentence. "For the remainder of your pregnancy. You will, naturally, have the finest medical care. I will import the finest obstetricians from around the globe and they will attend to you. Whatever you want, it will be yours. But you will stay here, out of sight. You will give birth to the child and I will make certain that you have all the care options any woman could want. Nannies, nurses, tutors. Neither you nor the child will lack for anything. And only after a suitable interval, when the child is older and the world has moved on from counting months and remembering old scandals, will it be permissible for you to do as you like." He considered, his eyes dark. "Within reason, of course."

The words didn't really make sense. Victoria studied him as best she could when everything inside her was flame and horror and passion and revolt, and she had no idea what expression was on her face. Something she knew better than to let happen when in the presence of a man who thought he ruled over her. In fact, she had not let it happen—even once—since she was a girl.

But she could only feel that hand at her throat and the mad din within her.

Whatever Ago saw on her face seemed to satisfy him well enough, for he nodded. In that curt way of his, that, Victoria realized, was mere punctuation to whatever decree he might have made. It indicated only that he, again, was finished with the topic at hand. It only *looked* as if he was interacting. It was only a gesture, pretending to be courteous when he was anything but.

So finished was he, in fact, that he was heading for the door.

Because he didn't require a conversation, she understood with a start. He had never intended to have one. He had delivered his intentions and that was all there was to it, by his reckoning.

Her pulse began to pound.

"Sorry," Victoria said, and it was a greater battle than she wanted to admit to keep her tone even. Or anything close to even, because she didn't think she'd quite made it there. "Did I hear you correctly? You intend to sequester me here? Lock me up and throw away the key...for years?"

Ago stopped, having drawn even with her seat on his way for the door. And he seemed to look down at her from a far greater height than his own six feet and then some. "I wish for you to disappear, Victoria."

"Is that..." She cleared her throat to *do something* about that phantom chokehold because it was that or succumb to...too many things to name, and she had the terrible fear that if she gave in to even one, she would be locking herself up and tossing away the key. Victoria couldn't allow that. "Is that a threat?"

A faint crease appeared on his noble brow. "A dead wife would hardly be less of a scandal."

She nodded sagely at that, and even managed to affect a somewhat thoughtful expression, as if this was all some kind of academic discussion. Instead of what sounded like a rather detailed plan for her life in exile. "But whenever you grant me permission to reemerge, many years from now, won't that cause its own scandal?"

"The truth is that you are considered so virtuous—or so overzealously policed by your father—that you already cause very few ripples," he told her, and Victoria had the distinct impression that he thought he was giving her some kind of compliment. When to her ears, it sounded a lot like he was suggesting she was invisible. Did he truly believe any woman wanted to hear that? "It is my wish that you simply…disappear beneath the waves entirely. When you reemerge, as you put it, it will be as a thirty-something mother of a child past the toddler years entirely. No one will care, and that will be an end to it. The important thing is to put distance between any whispers of my brother and the legitimacy of my heir."

How small she felt, with Ago peering down at her the way he was. The great man dispensing his judgment, her own wishes as insubstantial as the mist creeping in outside as the weather turned. Victoria had already lived like that. She did not intend to repeat the experience. She climbed to her feet as gracefully as she could under the circumstances.

Once she rose, she smoothed down her wedding gown, watching the way Ago's dark gaze

moved to her bump—to the child they'd made—
then away.

It should not have left her with the lingering
impression of heat, nor the stain of his hard kiss
upon her lips once more.

As if he'd left a mark.

"That's the matter of my confinement sorted,
then," she said, with a demure calm that had always soothed her father in his worst rages. She
even smiled, because she was good at that, too.
"A bit *Lion in Winter*, I grant you. But what of the
rest of our marriage?"

Ago's jaw tightened. She could see a muscle
flex there, and it was fascinating. More than fascinating. But she was not foolish enough to do
what everything in her yearned to do, and reach
out. She doubted very much that he would care
for it if she tried to touch him.

Instantly, that was the only thing she wanted
to do. So much so that it hurt—it actually *hurt*—
that she couldn't.

The way he studied her made her wish he really had locked her up in a tower, like the queen
in her favorite play.

"In many ways, Victoria," Ago said after a moment, in a voice that seemed to rumble through her
and around her, winding its way down the length
of her spine and then settling in that heated space
between her legs that only he had ever touched,

"you were, on paper, the perfect candidate to become my wife. I won't deny that I considered you for myself for some time. Long before I thought of you for my brother."

This, she was given to understand by the intensity of his expression and the timbre of his voice, was *not* a compliment.

"What an honor," she managed to murmur.

In a manner that he clearly did not find sarcastic, because he carried on speaking. "But it was quickly apparent to me that my brother's needs were the greater. And once you were linked to my brother, however tenuously, it would be scandalous to take you for my own."

Victoria was feeling slightly better now that she'd gotten to her feet, but she still hadn't quite reached the level of calm competence she preferred to feel when contending with domineering men. Still, if she knew anything in this life, it was to make use of what she had.

"Forgive me any impertinence," she said in as subdued a tone as she could manage, as if it was only out of the deepest politeness that she was not casting her eyes to the ground before him. Or casting herself down to tug at the cuff of his trouser, fully prostrate and obsequious, as she imagined men like him preferred. Her father certainly did. "But is that not exactly what happened in my uncle's garden?"

Again, that muscle in his jaw went wild. Beating much like her own pulse.

"It was my intention only to express my deepest apologies for what occurred—or did not occur—with Tiziano last Christmas," Ago bit out.

This time, she was not able to keep a rueful note from her voice. "So you said. Later that night."

With a certain ferocious anguish that she had spent months sifting through, in the privacy of her own thoughts.

"Today I've taken responsibility for my actions in a way that honors you, me, the Accardi legacy, and the child we have created," he told her, as if rendering a verdict. There was very little she could do but gaze back at him, that familiar panic mixing with a kind of astonishment inside of her, and tipping over. "But I am afraid, Victoria, that the kind of woman who would succumb to such indiscretions outside in a garden where anyone might have seen her is disqualified by definition from any true consideration to become the wife I imagined I would take."

"And yet I am your wife nonetheless," she said with great dignity, because it was that or point out the idiocy of what he just said to her. Then again, why not both? "Though it hardly seems fair that you blame me for something you took part in."

More than *took part in*, if she was being honest. Given that *she* hadn't known what she was doing.

It had been clear that he did.

"Make no mistake." And Ago's voice was as close to ragged as she had ever heard it, at least when he was not touching her. It almost made her imagine that he felt as she did, somewhere beneath his stern exterior—but she knew better than to allow herself such fantasies. "The fault is mine. The blame is also mine. I betrayed myself that night. And I will never forgive myself for the stain I have brought to bear upon my family's legacy with such a thoughtless, reckless act. I, who have dedicated the whole of my life to keeping my name and my honor washed clean."

"That seems a bit harsh," she found herself saying, though she knew it was unwise to argue with him. And then, as if that opened up the floodgates, she continued on when she knew the best strategy was silence and seeming acquiescence. "We can make the best of it, can't we? I always knew that a marriage—any marriage—was the only way to escape my father's hold. You said yourself that you once considered me a good candidate for the position I now occupy. Surely, somewhere between those two poles, a pleasant marriage that serves us both can exist. We need only be rational about this, surely."

Ago did not move any closer to her, and yet,

once again, the clatter of her own heart threatened to drown out the world. And the way he looked at her, almost too intent to bear, made everything in her seem to shake.

"Rational," he repeated, as if she'd hurled curses at him. "What, pray, do you consider a rational solution to this issue?"

"If the issue you're concerned about is the scandal," she said—quite reasonably, to her mind, "what scandal can there be now? The child is yours. I assume you had no doubts on that score, because you did not demand a battalion of tests."

An expression she could not begin to define moved over his beautiful face then, making it darker. Bleaker. "What does it matter what a test might say?" His voice was a harsh scratch over the space between them. "I know what I did that night."

Then, to her astonishment, he moved as if he meant to put his hands on her again. And everything inside her seemed to tilt and whirl about, spinning out in an overwrought sort of hope—

But he dropped his hand.

And she despaired of herself.

"Besides," Ago said, the bleakness that had been on his face now a heavy roughness in his voice, "I know full well that the only time your father ever permitted you to wander outside the sight of your guards was at your uncle's house.

And I also know that I'm the only guest your uncle has ever had while you were in residence. I am as reasonably secure in the fact you carry my heir as any man could be in the absence of a blood test. Which we will also be sure to conduct, *mia mogliettina*, never you fear. Just as soon as the appropriate medical team arrives. But we will do this quietly, far beyond the reach of any enterprising paparazzi."

"Wonderful," Victoria said with a serenity that cost her, especially when everything within her was still on fire with that longing for his touch. "I do like to remove doubt about my trustworthiness wherever possible."

Ago reached over then, his hard fingers a sudden brand against her chin. And she had wanted his touch, hadn't she?

You do, came a voice from within her. *No matter what kind of touch it might be.*

"There will be no doubt, Victoria," he said, his words quiet, but intense. His gaze alight. "One way or another, there will be no doubts between us at all. I promise you that."

He seemed to remember himself then, because he dropped his hand and stepped back, though all those sparks between them seemed to blaze all the higher.

Or maybe she was the one who could not keep herself from spontaneously combusting. Because

Ago turned and left the room, and despite the clamoring inside her that bordered on frantic, Victoria knew it was the better part of valor *not* to follow him.

Not to chase after him and beg for things she couldn't even name.

Because tonight was her wedding night and there was no need to sleep with the groom, because she'd already done that. Though there had been precious little sleeping indeed. And it was difficult not to marvel at how strong Ago had been and how he could lift her this way and that, so that she felt as light as a feather—

Another memory she did not need to dwell on.

So instead, Victoria sat back down in her seat at the foot of her new husband's table. And she ordered herself extra desserts when the staff made their way back in.

Because no one else might wish to celebrate what had happened today, but that didn't mean she couldn't.

She helped herself to an enormous slice of cake and dug in.

"Well, little bit," she murmured to the baby in her belly, "we had high hopes, it's true. But it turns out that all men really are the same." She forked in a mouthful of cake, chewed thoughtfully, then patted her belly. "If you're a boy, I apologize. I'm sure you'll be spectacularly unique."

And she polished off the rest of the cake. And the rest of the desserts too, because some women had bridesmaids, but Victoria had learned long ago to content herself with sugar and butter instead.

Happy wedding day to me, she thought later, when she was still on a sugar high but safely locked away in her charming little guest suite that was nowhere near Ago's rooms.

But the wedding wasn't what stayed foremost in her mind. Because what she couldn't help returning to from Ago's little rant on the subject of her *disappearance* was that he hadn't mentioned guards. When in her experience, men who planned to set guards on her liked to tell her so. And guards were the reason that Victoria had remained so seemingly biddable.

That and the fact that her father's whole intention was to give her to someone else, which would necessitate him no longer having the slightest say in what she did or where she went—so why fight it?

She had not anticipated that her new husband would suggest that she secrete herself in Tuscany for the remainder of her twenties, but again. The way he'd said it, he had seemed to suggest that he anticipated that she would obey him…simply because he was Ago Accardi? Or perhaps because he was used to asking for things and having them come true, fully formed, right there in front of him.

But as eager as Victoria might have been to marry her way out of her father's house, she had no intention of squandering any of her precious freedom now that she'd done so. That phase of her life was behind her.

And she had hoped that her husband would be reasonable, but hope was not the same thing as an appropriate plan. So while Ago spent the next week storming about the house, arranging things to his satisfaction, Victoria merely…bided her time.

She endured her father's company for a day or so before he apparently finished all the shouting he intended to do on a subject that was now, to her mind, moot. She was relieved when he drove off in his usual temper. For then it was a simple matter of wandering about the villa like a biddable cow, expressing no opinions and doing whatever was asked of her. Blood test? *Happy to oblige.* Required appearances at two meals a day? *How lovely.*

In those meals, Victoria did her best to act as bland and insipid as possible without arousing any suspicion so that, when a week had passed, Ago could remove himself from the family estate with every reason to suppose that the dull, boring paragon of sullied virtue he had married out of duty would just…stay where he'd put her.

Like an heirloom on a dusty shelf he might forget to look for again.

She waited another day or two, just to make sure that there were no secret guards lurking about the place, keeping themselves hidden until after the master's departure.

And then, a week and a half after marching down the aisle to marry the ferocious Ago Accardi, and with the blood test to prove that she absolutely was carrying his firstborn son, Victoria Cameron Accardi helped herself to one of the many cars in the villa's garages—because it wasn't stealing if they were married, was it?—and escaped.

CHAPTER FOUR

"Repeat yourself, please," Ago suggested, much too quietly, to his head of security.

The man stood before him, hat literally in hand and an expression on his face that Ago would have said could never possibly appear on the visage of a man who was his own army. Was that…contrition? Or even worse—panic?

"I'm terribly sorry, sir," the man said stiffly. "She abandoned the vehicle in Florence. We suspect she caught a train out of the city, but we're still chasing down any available camera footage that might give us a clue as to which direction she might have gone in."

Ago had been back in London for three days. He had finally gotten back to work. He had, mere moments before, congratulated himself with no small amount of relief that he was truly blessed. For despite the whisper of scandal attached to Victoria Cameron, and despite the glimpses here and there that he'd had of the real her beneath the layers of deference that had no doubt been bred in her from the start, she had settled into her new reality beautifully.

Which meant that he could compartmentalize to his heart's content and arrange the world as he saw fit. The way he always had done.

As if that woman, now his wife, made him feel nothing at all.

As if his remarkable divergence from his usual dutiful existence had never happened.

What his security chief was telling him made absolutely no sense.

"I'm having trouble understanding you," he said, though he certainly was not. "Are you truly suggesting that my wife fled the family estate and abandoned one of my vehicles on the streets of Florence? Like some kind of thief?"

"Her maids report that she took very few clothes with her, which could indicate that this is nothing more than a lark," the man replied. "Unfortunately, she also took her passport."

Ago pushed back from the great, wide desk that had been his father's and his grandfather's before him, and stood. He saw the man before him repress a flinch, and could only wonder what expression must be on his face that a former SAS officer thought he might take a swing at him.

But it also reminded him that his façade was

cracking, and he couldn't have that. He had not spent year after year crafting it into appropriate shape to let some foolish girl wreck him because she thought she was *on a lark*.

And especially because he did not, as policy, choose to engage with people who were not in the same room. Who were not even in the same country, damn her.

He turned abruptly and faced out the window. And though he knew London arranged itself prettily before him on this cold morning, he saw nothing.

Nothing, that was, except Victoria. The memories of her that plagued him and had chased him across half a year. This was all his fault. He knew that. And yet still he could not seem to keep himself from going over that night in the garden again and again.

He even knew why. He was desperate to cast her in the role of temptress. A terrible harlot when he knew full well that no other man had touched her. She had not needed to tell him. He was experienced enough to know that her charmingly astonished reactions to every touch, every kiss were not feigned.

It had all been new to her.

And what was new to him, all these months later, was that he could not seem to shake the ghost of her.

Not even marrying her and discovering that she did indeed carry his son, not even the old family house packed full of memories he usually avoided entirely, seemed to help.

"You may leave me," he told his security chief through a jaw that felt as if it might shatter at any moment. "I will expect an update within the hour."

"Yes, sir," came the immediate reply.

With a hint of relief, as if the man had expected Ago to rage and throw things.

As if that was an admonishment—and it certainly felt like one—Ago stayed where he was, staring out his wall of windows as if the City of London could provide him with some relief from this torment.

When he knew by now that there was no relief.

Because now it was worse. Now it was not simply need and heat in the dark. Now it was the sight of Victoria gliding toward him down that aisle in a chapel where Accardis had claimed their women for centuries. Now it was that roar inside him that he had tried so hard to deny, even as it happened. *Mine.*

It was that and it was all the rest of it. The way sunlight seemed to follow her from room to room even on a gray November day. The way she watched him, so carefully, so intensely, as if she was committing his every word and gesture to memory.

Because though she said nothing that was not polite and never set so much as a finger or a utensil wrong, she still got to him. And he had no idea what he was expected to do with the storm inside of him that he suspected would break free at the slightest provocation.

He had no idea how long he stood there, seeing nothing but her face. It might have been days—

But then the door to his office flew open behind him.

Ago gritted his teeth again, because there was only one person on the whole of the earth who would dare disturb his privacy at will.

Only one, and it was certainly not his deferential secretary.

"I do not recall inviting you in, brother," he growled. His younger brother's inappropriately raucous laugh grated, but then, he knew that Tiziano meant it to do just that.

"I am not a vampire, Ago. I don't require an invitation. Or have you forgotten? This is my company too."

"Even if I wished it," Ago muttered, "I could not possibly forget it."

Though he was not being entirely serious. There had been times when he'd doubted his brother's contributions to the family company, it was true. But in the past year, Tiziano had leveled up. He had proved that his haphazard successes, thrown about here and there accidentally, were in actuality the kind of marketing acumen that others paid excessive amounts to attempt to copy. Ago had learned that Tiziano had always wanted to be *seen* as haphazard and undependable. Now that he was in love and settled, he no longer felt the need to be seen as less than he was.

And Ago was not one to traffic in psychoanalysis, particularly of his younger brother. But he did enjoy that Tiziano took a far more active role in the company these days. He could admit that. Though not in his brother's presence, of course.

"I have heard the most extraordinary rumor," Tiziano told him, sloping into the room looking as he always did—like some kind of near-disreputable character who might have accidentally slept in the exquisite suit he wore, handcrafted for him, specifically, by one of the many couture houses who competed for his custom. "It involves our favorite *possibly* pregnant heiress. And, to my eternal astonishment, you."

"Where?" Ago asked shortly.

"In the bedroom with a bottle of wine?" Tiziano returned lazily. He laughed again, and it had precisely the same effect on Ago. "I assure you, brother, I do not require all the details of this scandalous event. I'm just flabbergasted that one occurred. Were you forced to participate? At gunpoint?"

"I meant, where did you hear such a rumor?"

Tiziano lounged his way across the room, then threw himself into the chair across from Ago's desk, looking entirely boneless.

Ago knew he did it for the express purpose of driving Ago up the wall. And he hated that he was so on edge that it worked.

"Are you denying it?" Tiziano asked, a gleam of amusement in his gaze.

"I never comment on tabloid nonsense. You know this."

"But it was not in a tabloid," Tiziano murmured, looking entirely too pleased with himself. "I heard this from no greater authority than our dear cousin Patricio, who claims to have married you himself."

Ago sighed. He had a set of wholly uncharacteristic urges course through him, then. To run his fingers through his hair, when he kept it close-cropped enough that there could be no profit in it. To fiddle and fidget, like he was some boy stood before a headmaster—or his own disapproving father and grandfather.

The Accardi heir had never been allowed such indications that he might be like everyone else. He had never been permitted to be normal.

"Patricio is correct," he said, because he had

also never been permitted to faff about with flowery language like his brother. He had been expected to reply with the correct answer, and succinctly, or risk a swift punishment. "We are married."

He said this very shortly, and with a glare—not that this in any way discouraged his brother.

"I am shocked and appalled," Tiziano drawled, while looking and sounding neither. "How can this be? Do you mean to tell me you had a wedding and failed to invite your favorite and only brother?"

Ago sighed again. "You already know that I did. It is why you are here today, I can only assume."

"I do know you did," Tiziano agreed merrily. "What I don't know is why you married in secret. Very much as if you have something to hide."

And Ago thought then that he would prefer to launch himself through his windows to the streets far below than continue this conversation. The speculation in Tiziano's gaze made him consider it.

"You will be delighted to hear that I am, after all, a mortal and fallible man like any other," he managed to grit out, though it caused him literal pain. "But I have taken responsibility for my failings."

He stood as straight as he could, and found the

play of expressions he couldn't quite read over his brother's face unbearable.

"Let me make certain I'm understanding you, brother," Tiziano said, his voice a lazy drawl. Which meant he was primed and ready to lean into the mockery he was so good at.

But Ago found that he was finished with this conversation.

"Spare me, please, the schadenfreude," he growled. "How the mighty have fallen, and so on. I have said all of these things to myself, and more. I'm sure that, in time, I will learn to live with what I have done."

His younger brother studied him as if he made no sense.

"Felicitations," he said. After a very long moment. "That sounds very much like love's young dream. Romantic to the extreme. Lucky Victoria."

Ago thought he could hear his own teeth grinding together. "I know nothing of romance and have no plans to learn," he told his younger brother icily. "What I know is responsibility. I abdicated my own but briefly, and now must pay the price. That is all there is to it."

Though it did occur to him, as he made such sweeping statements, that his supposedly biddable bride was even now gallivanting about Europe. Flashing the proof of the scandal he would prefer to hide away everywhere she went.

And that was all it would take to start a landslide of gossip.

This was what happened, Ago knew. This was what his grandfather and father had warned him about, again and again. All it took was one little slip. One mistake, and then everything else was a slippery slope straight on into utter disgrace.

This was why he had never made any mistakes.

The only question now was whether or not he could stave off the worst potential consequences. Because so far, a few desultory rumors were the only evidence of his sin.

All he needed to do was locate and collect his bride, and this time, not foolishly assume that the obedience she had showed her father would automatically transfer to her husband. He ought to have been grateful. Because now, he knew precisely where he stood and would not forget it.

Yet he found that *grateful* was not at all how he felt.

"Ago." He had almost forgotten that Tiziano still lounged there before him. Almost. "You do know that Victoria is…a person. A woman, now pregnant, who is possessed of all her own thoughts, and emotions, needs and wishes and hopes. As the baby will be when it is born. And most people on this earth are not as amenable as you have always been to hiding themselves away in a very small, steel-lined box."

"Thank you, Tiziano," Ago said, forbiddingly. "For demonstrating to me, yet again, the difference between us. The box around me, as you put it, is called duty. It is steel-lined indeed, little as I think you know what that means."

And though his brother laughed, Ago had the strangest notion that he'd…missed something here. An opportunity, perhaps, to have a different relationship than the one he and Tiziano had always had. The opportunity to be more than the heir and the spare, which was all they had ever been raised to be.

Not exactly the closest relationship, he could admit.

But all he could think about was the scandal that could even now be making its way into every tabloid paper in Europe, branding Ago as no better than any other too-human fool. When he had worked so hard, and sacrificed everything, to never, ever put so much as a foot wrong. To be something more than a man.

An Accardi, his grandfather thundered inside him, *cannot lower himself to be something so prosaic as a mere* man.

He wanted to rage at his brother. Or better still, Victoria herself.

But he knew, down deep, that the real villain in this was himself.

That was what made it so difficult to bear.

He decided to abstain from any more of Tiziano's witticisms. Or worse still, the way that his brother's dark gaze, so much like his own, turned too knowing for his tastes. Ago took the opportunity to quit the room, leaving Tiziano behind in his office as he stalked down the hallways of Accardi Industries' sleek headquarters, taking no particular pleasure in the way the very sight of him sent his underlings into their usual flutter.

He ignored the secretaries in a tizzy and the junior executives who flattened themselves against the wall, eyes wide, as he passed. He marched down to the security chief's office and was gratified when the man met him at the door.

"I trust the situation is already close to being resolved?" Ago asked thinly.

"There is good news," the man replied, looking less panicked than before. That had to indicate progress, surely. "We think she's in Cinque Terre."

And it was a measure of how disquieted Ago was that he didn't pounce on the word *think*.

Instead, he pulled out his mobile, punched out his personal assistant's number, and began issuing orders.

But though the claims that Victoria had been in Cinque Terre seemed legitimate, they soon discovered that she did not stay there. And it was not clear in the days that followed whether Ago's errant wife knew that she was being followed and was leading them all in a merry chase, or if she was simply, carelessly, crisscrossing her way across the Italian boot.

She followed no set routine. She made no reservations. It was as if she simply woke up wherever she found herself and then wandered about wherever the day took her—whether it was getting on a train because it happened to stop near her, or checking in to a *pensione* because she happened to be passing one on an old medieval street. They tracked her from the seaside villages of Cinque Terre inland to Lucca's medieval walls and steaming bowls of *tortelli lucchese*, then off to the mysteries of Venice.

Ago had been so certain that she would be caught quickly that he had left London and headed to the Accardi estate. But days later, he found himself in the back of one of his SUVs as the security chief himself drove them in and out of hill towns and villages. Ravenna, Perugia, Naples, and the Amalfi coast.

Was he truly reduced to chasing after a woman in this way? It seemed impossible and yet here he was. He, Ago Accardi, who had never pursued a woman in his life, brought to such lows. He was having trouble accepting not only that, but the fact that a sheltered girl who had never been let out on her own could elude his entire security force for more than two hours. Much less for nearly two weeks.

He was going to have to review his security arrangements—but first he had to find his wife.

It was a great victory when they tracked her, at last, to Rome. And better still, to a specific hotel in the Eternal City that catered to those with privacy concerns. She'd been thoughtful enough to take a floor to herself and enjoyed the convenience of her own entrance, which meant that Ago did not have to concern himself with being recognized in any kind of hotel lobby.

Better still, she stayed put for more than a night.

They followed her as she wandered through the neighborhood on her second day in Rome, stopping at a café and then wandering with what looked like simple, aimless pleasure through the old streets. As if she had not absconded for any reason at all, other than taking in the sights.

Ago found himself in the blackest temper he could recall.

When he did not let loose his temper, ever. It was just another form of passion, dangerous and unwieldy.

He rather thought he blamed her for that, too, as he found himself in the street that night, glaring balefully up at her windows. But nothing was to be gained from indulging either one. As he already knew, to his peril. So he stood longer than necessary, out there in the cold Roman street, forcing himself to search for some semblance of calm. To take one breath, then another, until that rapid pounding of his blood eased.

Or eased somewhat, anyway.

Only when he was reasonably certain that he could contain himself did he move, going around the side of the deliberately unmarked if quietly elegant building and following the small alley that led to three separate staircases, one for each floor. He took the final one, knowing it led to the top floor and to his wife.

His wife.

It was funny how those words seemed to rush through him, tonight. As if he'd never heard them or thought them before. Or as if it was different, now, somehow. Because he had hunted her for near on two weeks. And so it seemed the culmination of a great many things, tonight.

Through six months he had waited, assuming that not hearing from her at all had meant that somehow, he had been saved from the consequences of his actions that night in her uncle's garden.

Only to discover that he had not been saved at all.

There was only one thing left to save. His good name and what remained of his reputation, once unsullied, now that so many rumors had been let loose to fly about as they would. He supposed he would simply have to live with the fact that Tiziano knew the unsavory truth.

Though that might be the bitterest pill of them all.

He found his way to Victoria's door, pausing to consider with no little contempt the difference between *private* and *secure*. A vast gulf that Victoria would never have to concern herself with again, for he intended to see that she never set foot off of his property as long as she lived—

But that could wait. Here and now, he raised his hand and pounded on her door with his fist.

For long moments, there was nothing. He could feel Rome all around him, and though he had always loved the city, he found he resented it tonight. So many lives humming all around him now and stretching back thousands of years, and yet here he was, consumed with doing his best to stop his own downward spiral before it took him over. Like some kind of nameless, pointless ant.

Perhaps the real truth was that it didn't seem fair. Maybe that was what he resented most, because who had dedicated themselves to duty and family honor more than he had? How had he come to this?

But, of course, he knew.

More long moments passed, and he was about

to pound on the door once more when he heard the locks turn. She did not ask who was there, another point he would need to raise in future.

And then suddenly the door was thrown open, and she was there.

"I'm so sorry, I don't think I called for any—" she began, but then stopped dead.

And Ago watched with what he told himself was the greatest disinterest as the color left her face, and her summer blue eyes widened.

"Ago…" she breathed.

"The very one," he replied coldly.

But he did not wait for her to invite him inside. He strode forward, expecting her to fall back, and so she did. With a deepening flush on her porcelain cheeks, reminding him that she had been meant to be not only the perfect English rose, but an innocent in every respect.

Instead of the kind of woman who would lead her husband on a merry chase against his specific instructions.

"I have spent the past two weeks tracking you this way and that across the Italian peninsula," he told her shortly as he found his way down the hall that led off of the entryway and into the room where she must have been sitting, for it was bright with light, the flat-screen television on the wall had been paused, and it smelled of her. He gritted his teeth. "When I distinctly recall making it clear to you that I wished for you to remain where I left you."

She watched him with what he thought was wariness and he told himself he was glad of it. Because she should be wary. She should be terrified, in fact, and flutter about like one of his secretaries, halfway to hysterics at the very idea that she might have disappointed him.

But Victoria did not appear to be the fluttering type. She followed him into the salon, and her hands found her hips, somewhere behind the heft of her pregnancy bump.

"You made a great many things clear, Ago," she said, and though she was agreeing with him, it was evident from the way she was looking at him that this was not going to be a reprise of the biddable bride he now suspected had been a fantasy all along. "But I never had any intention of celebrating my escape from my father's clutches by locking myself away again. I'm pretty sure I told you that."

"You are pregnant with my heir," he bit out. "Your childish fantasies of escape no longer apply."

She studied him for a moment, then dropped her hands from her hips, moving further into the room. "There's a hiking path in Cinque Terre. You can climb up high and look out at the bright, happy villages clinging to the hills. I've seen pictures of it my whole life. How could I not go and see it myself?"

"The Accardi estate boasts many walking trails," he replied, his voice dark. "I suggest you avail yourself of them."

"In Venice, I waded across St. Mark's Square and ate gelato on a gondola. In Ravenna I took walking tours and learned about Etruscans, Gauls, and the Byzantine Empire. I ate chocolate in Perugia and dreamed of endless summers in Amalfi."

"I don't require your itinerary, Victoria. I have been on your heels this whole time."

That seemed to neither discomfit nor intrigue her. She only shrugged. "Would you believe that every place I've been lived up to and then surpassed every expectation I had? I could have stayed in each new place forever. But how could I? Because for the first time in my life, I have no one to answer to. Nowhere to go. No one chasing after me with an agenda and harsh expectations of what I should do and when. It's been liberating."

"And what do you suppose the cost of this liberation is?" But what Ago was focused on was the fact that he should not have come so far to this room. Because she had followed him and was now too close.

And with the notable exception of their wedding day, he had gone to great lengths to make sure that he was never too close to Victoria again.

This was problematic.

She was problematic.

Even here in a Roman hotel, drenched in her perfidy, she still smelled like lilacs and cream. And his body had an immediate and devastating response.

When the last thing in the world he needed right now was to be reminded of how he'd gotten himself into this predicament in the first place.

He opened his mouth to continue one of his lectures, the kind that would make his brother sigh and roll his eyes dramatically. But instead, all that lilac and cream seemed to blend together with memories, making everything worse. Because her skin was so soft, and he knew precisely where he could put his mouth at the crook of her neck to make her shudder. Her kisses had been artlessly enthusiastic, and it made that storm in him rage anew to remember how quickly she learned what he taught her. How to fence with him, her tongue in his. How to angle her head and move closer.

And then, later, there on a bench in her uncle's garden, he had taught her how to find her pleasure first with his fingers, then with his sex, and how to cover her sobs by letting him drink them from her lips.

He was having a hard time remembering why he had come here tonight.

Because it was one thing to avoid temptation

as a matter of course his whole life. It was something else again to know and remember every last second of it, and ask himself why on earth he was resisting now.

"The thing about liberation," Victoria said softly, "is that it is worth any cost."

His sex ached, but he focused instead on her words.

"I'm grateful to you, *mia mogliettina*, for proving to me, beyond any doubt, who you are," he told her with a certain grimness. "You are not to be trusted. You cannot be depended upon. Any hopes I might have had that there was something to salvage in this situation of ours are gone."

He expected her to wither at that, as so many would have. He did not often bring out the full force of his disapproval because he knew perfectly well that people found him unbearably stern. They crumbled before him like so much ash in the wind.

But surely the situation called for it.

He waited for Victoria to crumble before him.

But instead, to his intense shock, poor, sheltered Victoria...

Laughed.

Laughed. At *him*.

He could hardly believe it.

And yet on she laughed, as if he was a figure of fun. It tempted him to feel something very nearly murderous instead.

But Victoria, his wife who in no way seemed to know her place...kept right on laughing.

As if daring him to *do* something about it.

CHAPTER FIVE

VICTORIA DIDN'T MEAN to laugh, but before she knew it the laughter took her over. And then it was like she was carried away by the force of it and even when she tried, she couldn't seem to stop.

Especially when the implacable, merciless Ago stared at her in stunned amazement. Affront written all over him.

Just in case she wondered if anyone had dared laugh at him before.

Any other man would have looked ridiculous. Even pitiable, so out of his arrogant depth. But not Ago.

Never Ago.

Victoria had opened the door thinking it was the front desk, because the hotel was lovely and attentive, and had instead literally been struck dumb at the sight of him. He was somehow bigger than she remembered, blocking out the overhead light as he stood there on the landing outside her door, glowering in obvious fury while his dark blue eyes were so intense it nearly hurt.

She probably should have attempted to bar his way, but she hadn't been able to summon up the will to do it. Not when her heart was clamoring in her chest and her traitorous body flushed all over. And now they were standing in this hotel room together, which seemed…decadent, at best. Not to mention foolish.

And also unbearably intimate, because here in this hotel with that heavy front door closed tight, they were truly alone.

When they hadn't been alone together, not really. Not in all this time. There had been guards milling about within shouting range and her uncle and all the rest of his household staff six months ago. Then her father had been seemingly omnipresent when she'd arrived in Italy, and had continued to storm about after the wedding, too. Even after her father had taken himself back to England, there had still been Ago's staff. Bustling all around the ancient estate to make certain that the Accardi in residence had whatever he might need or want before he needed or wanted it.

This, right now, was the first time they had ever truly been on their own.

A kind of fizzy panic had bubbled up from deep inside her at the idea of any kind of *salvage operation* and she had no choice but to laugh it out. It was that or lose herself in it the way she had in his arms months ago.

She couldn't have stopped if her life depended on it, and maybe it did.

"Do you find this amusing?" Ago asked, his voice like a sharp sword that cut straight to the beating, fizzy heart of that panic. Victoria pulled in a ragged breath, not sure if she was *grateful* he'd cut her off—or something else entirely.

The sudden silence seemed to throb in her ears, expanding inside her like a terrible balloon. And for all he held himself still and straight, she could see the wildness in his dark blue gaze and she knew that, as ever, there were storms in him. Just there, just beneath his skin.

It was her curse that she felt compelled to dance in them.

Victoria moved closer tonight, because now she'd had time. Time on her own for the first time in her life. True time to herself without having to answer to anyone. She did not have to account for her time, her fancies, her interests. She did not have to discuss her whims with anyone or accept it when what she wanted was denied her with little or no explanation. Instead, for once, she had simply wandered as the spirit took her and done exactly as she liked.

And she had found that in the absence of her father's usual overbearing behavior and bullying remarks—and freed now of the gnawing fear that had consumed her for months that her pregnancy would be discovered at any moment—she had spent entirely too much time thinking about Ago.

And not just reliving the night in her uncle's garden that had brought her here.

Victoria had spent her nights of freedom, tucked up in charming inns and slick hotels all over Italy, researching the man who happened to be her husband. In a manner she'd never allowed herself to do before. Because first, she was certain that her father's staff spied on her in any number of ways, including tracking what she did online. And second, because it seemed inappropriate to look up Ago when it had been made very clear to her that she was meant for his brother. And no one ever had to look up Tiziano. His exploits were splashed everywhere, for all to see, night and day.

Tiziano would have been a friendly, easy affair, she'd thought. That was all he had to offer. And if she found herself dreaming instead of the older Accardi brother—the one who actually spoke to her and made her heart pound with the intensity of his regard—that was one of the only secrets she got to keep to herself.

Though after that Christmas season last year, when Tiziano had made such a scene with his mistress that Victoria had felt compelled to tell Ago herself that there could be no engagement, she found herself a little *too* focused on the sterner, darker, more overwhelming Accardi.

It was his fault, because surely he should have known better than to stand so close to her at that Christmas Eve gala. He had been the experienced one. She had felt like nothing so much as a boat tossed about by the tide.

Victoria had spoken to Tiziano's mistress herself earlier that night, and had found Annie Meeks nothing short of delightful. The kind of woman she would have liked for a friend, if she'd been allowed any. In one short conversation, Annie had made Victoria laugh and had made it clear that she loved Tiziano Accardi in a way that Victoria would have said no one could. But most importantly, in a way Victoria—who had expected to announce her engagement to Tiziano that very night—certainly didn't.

So she'd sought out Ago—who, while ferociously unyielding in all ways was still more approachable than her father—and told him that she couldn't possibly marry a man who was so recklessly and publicly in love with another woman.

I don't have a tremendous ego, she had told him, smiling serenely despite the fact that standing so close to the man, the singular focus of his intense gaze, had made her…sweat. *The nuns in the convent made sure of that. But I really must draw the line somewhere.*

That was the first time Ago had looked at her with all of that brooding, seething disappointment.

And somehow, she hadn't run away. She hadn't laughed, the way she'd been unable to keep herself from doing tonight.

Instead, her heart had done something astonishing in her chest while her stomach had seemed to plummet down to find the hem of her festive gown where it hit the floor. She had sucked in a breath, not sure where that riot inside of her had come from.

It would be all well and good if he was in love with no one, including me, she had told Ago, who had continued to stare down at her in such dark disapproval. *But to marry a man who's obviously capable of love? And, in fact, in love with someone else? I'm afraid I can't do it.*

Love, Miss Cameron, Ago had replied in freezing tones that the hint of Italy in his voice did nothing to melt, *is for silly teenage girls and foolish poets. I was led to believe you were a woman of sense.*

I have enough sense to step out of the path of a speeding train, I hope, Victoria had replied with sheer bravado, because she'd been standing stockstill as she stared up at Ago Accardi, hadn't she? *Because it's all very well to stand about talking of these bloodless marriages. But at the end of the day, it's still my life. And I have no illusions about the kind of life my father wants for me, Mr. Accardi. But I do still have to live it.*

The band had been playing Christmas standards and she'd felt them swell all around her as she'd stood there, lost somewhere in the darkest, most tumultuous blue of Ago's gaze.

And when she thought back, that was all she could remember of that conversation. It wasn't at all clear to her how she'd survived it.

Which was funny, because her father had spent the whole of that Christmas and well into the New Year, soundly abusing her for failing to catch Tiziano's interest. She shouldn't have remembered anything having to do with Ago Accardi with anything but a little bit of distaste and an overarching sense of injustice.

And then, of course, there had been that night at her uncle's house. When she'd been enjoying what passed for her freedom in those days by wandering around the gardens that evening, only to come face-to-face with him.

She still shuddered, thinking of it.

And what she'd discovered over the past week was that, left to her own devices, those were the moments she dwelled upon. Set free at last from all these men who worked so hard to keep her in this or that box of their choosing, she returned to those moments again and again. She still found herself going back to the gala. To that first moment in the garden.

To this impossible, immovable mountain of a man who should have scared her—but the way he made her shiver had nothing to do with fear.

Particularly not when she had increasingly had such scalding dreams, night after night, of exactly how she'd come to find herself pregnant.

Now, standing in this hotel room in Rome, she was happy that she'd spent so many hours over the past week familiarizing herself with all things Ago. It made her feel a little less at sea in his presence when she knew full well he'd had whole dossiers on *her*. And she didn't need anyone to tell her that it was best to have as many weapons as possible when facing a man like this. She knew.

She liked to think she'd always known.

All of this stormed through her, with and without the uncontrollable laughter, in the moments after *he* dared to tell *her* that *she* was not to be trusted.

"You set out your expectations for our marriage, I'll agree," she said carefully, testing to see if her body would betray her and set her laughing out her panic anew. Had he really suggested he thought there was something salvageable in exiling her in a country that wasn't even her own? "But I have expectations of my own, Ago.

And I see no particular reason why yours should take precedence."

"Do you not?" he asked, again in tones of the deepest, affronted amazement. Tones that she thought did not quite match the way he looked at her, in a manner that made her very nearly breathless—and reminded her too much of the garden that night. "I did not take you for a simpleton, Victoria."

She didn't react to that, but only because she had the distinct sense that he wanted her to. "We both know that my father's only goal was to sell me. I know he used other terms, but at the end of the day, that's what he was about. There's no point pretending otherwise."

"I have never pretended a day in my life." And again, despite what he said, all she could hear in his voice were echoes of that night. As if he was fighting with himself, somewhere deep inside. Maybe she only wished he was. "I would like it if you could extend me the same courtesy."

"I'm not pretending anything. But this isn't the situation my father expected to marry me into." She put her hands on her belly, in case he had somehow missed it, rounding out between them. And perhaps because she wanted to remind him how, exactly, this had come to pass. "I'm not going to blame you for what happened between us in that garden—"

"I should certainly hope not." This time, his voice had become a dark growl, so that all she could think of was the sound of that growl at her ear while he moved inside her. "Because my distinct recollection is that you were the one who threw yourself at me."

"And you are Ago Accardi," she replied, shaking her head at him. "I doubt it's possible for you to spend any time at all in public without women flinging themselves at you. If you'd wanted to set me aside, I feel certain you could have. And would have."

Once again, memories of that night seemed to flare between them. The way she had surged into his arms, overwhelmed yet *alight*, and determined that no matter what happened, she would not allow the moment to pass. She would not take another breath without tasting something more than the same old stale air of the cage she'd lived in all her life…

She was certain he was remembering the very same thing.

She could see the same flare of heat and need in his gaze.

But his voice was cool. "The fact remains that I was not the one who started us down this path, Victoria."

"Yet here we are," she said, no matter how

much she might have liked to stop and parse the things he said and fight him about it.

She knew better.

Life had taught her all manner of things so far, but perhaps nothing so keenly as the utter pointlessness arguing with men who had already made up their minds.

Even if—especially if—she thought they were lying to themselves.

"The only point I'm trying to make is that you didn't purchase my father's famously virginal daughter that he's been hawking for years. Our marriage isn't about innocence at all. It's about righting a wrong." When his eyes only blazed at her, all that longing and too many memories, she tapped her belly. "The supposed stain on my honor, which I think we both know means, on my father's pride."

Ago studied her until she felt…itchy.

But her years in convent schools meant she knew better than to show her reactions to such severe regard. No matter how difficult it was to stand there and gaze back at him tranquilly, she did it.

When he spoke, his voice was a dark silk, woven through with a distinct sort of threat that made everything inside her seem to shift. "I have no idea why you think that a reasonable response to forcing me to hunt you down as you flitted about the country, heedless of your own safety and that of the child you carry, is to stand here before me and tell me things I already know."

"Because you don't seem to have drawn the appropriate conclusions," she returned, still with the exaggerated calm and *reasonableness* that she, personally, considered her trademark. "I don't owe you anything, Ago. I could have refused to marry you. And for all my father's carrying on, it's not as if he was going to reel in the sort of great men he imagined I would marry while I was pregnant with your child. I could have gone the single parent route."

There was a part of her, she could admit, who had hoped that her father might toss her out—so she could do as she pleased and raise her child how she wished. No need to share her pregnancy with Ago. No need to involve any men at all.

Ago only lifted a dark brow, as if he knew exactly what she'd hoped. "There is no scenario in which any woman would ever be raising my child as a single parent of any kind."

There was something about the way he said that. It made Victoria swallow, hard. "What matters is that scandal has already happened and can't be fixed. Your worst nightmare has occurred and so has my father's. There's no taking any of it back." She made herself stand a little bit taller, then hated herself for needing to. "And it seems to me that instead of concerning myself with the dark imaginings of the two of you, I should, at last, concern myself with what *I* want."

"That is this freedom you speak of?" He folded his arms in a way that made the back of her neck prickle, so at odds was it with that heated thing in his gaze. The one she recalled too well from that long-ago night. "Why am I unsurprised to discover that your notion of freedom involves traipsing about in an irresponsible fashion, spending someone else's money, and considering it heroic? That is a hallmark of your generation, is it not?"

That stung. And she hated that it stung. It wasn't as if she'd been allowed to cross a street on her own, much less head out and make her own way in the world, was it? All she'd ever had before now were daydreams and private fantasies—the only things she could keep to herself.

But she focused on the swipe at her youth. "You're not exactly my father's age, Ago. You might want to rethink the generation talk."

"The same attitude permeates everything these days," Ago said, moving his hand in a motion that would have been a languid wave from anyone else. Yet nothing about this man was languid. "It is selfish and hedonistic. My own brother is guilty of it. But unfortunately for you, Victoria, you have put yourself into a position that, by its very nature, excludes you from such self-centered behavior."

Once again, the intensity of his gaze, the stern set of his mouth, seemed to pierce straight through her. And, to her shame, made that same old heat bloom deep within her. "The mother of the next Accardi heir cannot wander about at will. *My wife* cannot pretend, for even a moment, that she is in any way common. And before you accuse me, this has nothing to do with ego or pride. It is a simple fact that you, alone and in your current state, are a target. Maybe you think nothing of risking yourself. But you should think about the fact that your life is no longer only your own."

And, suddenly, it was unimaginable to her that she had ever laughed in this man's presence. Much less moaned in pleasure. She cradled her belly as if *from* him. "I know that you're not trying to stand here and lecture me on what it means to be pregnant with a child. I know that not even you would dare."

"It's time to grow up, Victoria." The way he said that was nothing short of a slap. "In a few short months you will be a mother. And I have no idea what kind of mother raised you—"

"I think you know perfectly well that my mother died when I was small. So if you have concerns about my upbringing, I suggest you raise them with your good friend and business associate. My father."

He ignored that. "My child requires a mother

of impeccable breeding with an attention to duty and a willingness to put our son above all else. That means, *mia mogliettina*, that there can be no more assignations in dark gardens. Or even the faintest hint of them."

Her jaw actually dropped at that. "I have had one assignation in my entire life, and it was with you. I doubt very much that you can say the same!"

"No gardens," he said again, very much as if he was handing down rules. As if this was the convent all over again, and no matter that she could see the heat in his gaze. "No indiscriminate appearances, flashing your pregnant belly for all the world to see. And certainly no childish disobedience, willfully rebelling for no better reason than to indulge some immature longing for wanderlust."

She was finding it hard to breathe as she glared back at him. "You sound like Mother Superior. Yet I am certain I graduated some years back."

That look in his dark gaze shifted, though she could not have said how. Only that she could feel it, deep within. A new flame, brighter than before.

"I am sorry that your life has not been as you wish it to be, Victoria. Truly, I am. But neither one of us has any justification to bemoan the life that could have been." And now the faint hint of something like softness she'd heard in his voice was gone as if it had never been. While that fire in him only seemed to burn cold. "We were both in that garden, as you pointed out. We both participated in the making of our child. And so we both will pay this penalty."

Victoria had to fight to stay calm. "And what if I don't want my life, or this marriage, or my child's upbringing to be a *penalty*, Ago?"

She fully expected him to blaze at her in a temper, or growl at her again. Or to coldly express his further astonishment at her temerity. Maybe even to give in to that heat she could sense in him, whether cold or blazing hot. But instead, he only looked at her as if he…couldn't understand what she meant.

Not as if she wasn't making sense, but as if he truly couldn't conceive of any of those things unless they were some or other form of punishment.

And she couldn't tell what it was—deep inside of her where she felt him in ways she couldn't explain, that had nothing to do with what had happened between them in that garden—that broke a bit at that. Only that it did. It shattered, and that what followed was an emotion she dared not name.

"There is more to life than an endless parade of brutal penalties, Ago," she said softly. Because there had to be, surely.

He smiled then—though really, it was simply

a twist of his hard mouth. There was no joy in it. Nothing close.

And that made what had broken in her seem to crumble all the more.

"You are welcome to think so." His voice was so dark. Too dark. "I can't stop you. But when it comes to the duty we owe to both the Accardi name and who will inhabit it one day, I must insist that you do as I say."

"And if I refuse?"

He shook his head at her, though again, his eyes were far too dark. "Unfortunately for you, *mia mogliettina*, you showed your hand already. Do you really believe that I will ever leave you to your own devices again? Do you imagine that I will ever trust you or anything you say to me, from this day forward? I will not. And if that means that you must spend your life under guard, well..." His shrug was as expansive as it was dismissive. "You will not be the first Accardi wife to live in this fashion. My earliest ancestors achieved peace and annexed land by taking brides from rival families. How do you think they managed it?"

Victoria had all those emotions swirling about inside her. And deeper still, that drumbeat of what she wanted to call temper, but was terribly afraid was something else. Something more in line with those mad dreams she had at night and the images that seduced her as she slept. Then haunted her well into the afternoon.

She had spent all her virginal years imagining what it would be like to have sex. And shoring up her imagination with a judicious bit of research, books, and films. She'd been fairly sure she was ready. As ready as any innocent could be, that was.

And still Ago Accardi had taken her into his arms and taught her that she knew nothing at all about want or need or longing until that night.

It was tempting to blame all the emotions she'd had since that night on her pregnancy, but deep down, she knew better. Even if she wasn't pregnant, she'd feel the things she did around him. All of them.

He would have haunted her all the same.

"Will you lock me in a tower, then?" she demanded, and her voice was no longer quite as calm and cool as she liked. "Will you throw away the key, or simply have a rotation of guards? Will I be forced to grow my hair long and bold and sing pointless songs out the window, hoping someone happens by to save me?"

He looked at her as if she were mad, as if he'd never read a fairy tale in his life. And instead of taking that as more evidence against him, more clues she needed to harden her position and refuse to obey him, it…made her heart hurt.

It made her wonder exactly what kind of childhood this man had had, that seemed to have involved nothing that any child should ever have to suffer. His whole life had been gilt-edged, to be sure. But beneath all that shine, all she seemed to find was sorrow.

Maybe that was why Victoria dared to draw closer to him. To put herself right there, in front of his folded arms, as close as she could get to him without her belly brushing up against him.

"I don't have any intention of spending another minute of my life locked up," she told him solemnly. "You can trust me or not trust me, whatever suits. And I can certainly bide my time if necessary. But I do not intend to remain any man's prisoner."

And yet somehow, this close to him, she no longer felt the same driving need to *make him understand.* Instead, she could smell the very hint of the cologne he wore, that she had only discovered that night in the garden. When she had been so close to him that the fact he smelled so wonderful had practically knocked her off her feet. And it was more dangerous tonight. Because the longer she stood there, the more his gaze seemed to change. It showed her more of that storm in him, but laced through with that same heat she could feel like a humming deep inside her.

"If you want me to obey you, Ago, you should try asking nicely."

Victoria forgot where they were, then. Because all she could see was him, and the way the fire inside him seemed to take over the whole of his gaze. She could see only him, and she knew this feeling too well. She'd felt it before. In a ballroom in London. A garden in Cornwall. The chapel in Tuscany.

As if Ago was the world.

And she could feel that tension between them, so hot and so bright that felt like some kind of electric current. And made her wonder how she ever...*didn't* feel it. For surely it was always here, drawing her to him. Making her aware of him in a way she was aware of no other man, no other person, alive.

Making her lean closer when by any reckoning, she should have wanted to run in the opposite direction. She should at least have *tried*.

Ago reached over and slid his palm over her cheek, as if outlining the line of her jaw. He moved up to her temple, then back down to her chin.

Victoria felt a wild heat, and it was not contained simply to the place he touched. Instead it raced through her like more of that same electricity, finding every place he'd ever touched, making her a living map of the passion they shared. Her collarbone. Her neck. The slopes of her breasts, and the nipples that even now tightened until she was nearly uncomfortable. A straight, breathtakingly hot line from the hollow between her breasts straight down between her legs, making her somehow feel as alive and delicate and *herself* as she'd been six months ago. Before her body had changed and the baby within her had taken her over.

Most of all, she felt him there between her legs, an ache that nothing made right or better. She could feel him in a line of delirious sensation all the way down her legs, deep into her toes, even as she curled them beneath her.

But it was there, in her feminine core, she wanted him most. Where everything was more intense than it had ever been, perhaps because she was not only pregnant, but pregnant with *his* baby, or so it seemed to her at that moment. All he needed to do was look at her like this and her whole body came to attention as if to shout, *look at how obedient I am. Look at how well I loved you that night, that I took all you gave me, and made new life.*

The look on his face changed, so that she almost thought she'd said those things out loud. And she recognized that glittering, deep blue and dangerous in all the best ways.

He found her lips and traced them. One way, then back.

And when he moved his hand yet again, a rough, hot caress that she could feel course through her, Victoria opened up her mouth and sucked his thumb in. She was aware that what she did was sensual and provocative, even though she'd never performed the act she knew was meant to mimic.

But she could see he recognized it all the same.

"Always such a greedy little thing, aren't you?" he asked, his voice a rough scrape of sound. It made her feel abraded, and she liked it. She licked the tip of his thumb and he grinned, a dark promise. "No wonder your father kept you locked away."

Before she could protest that—before she could tell him that she had never felt the slightest bit of greed for any man alive, save him—

Before she could do anything at all, Ago pulled his thumb from between her lips, and then crashed his mouth to hers.

CHAPTER SIX

IF KISSING HER was a mistake, Ago could not find it in himself to care the way he knew he should. The way he suspected he would once he quit the temptation of her nearness.

Because something about this woman roused him as none other ever had, no matter how he tried to fight it. The ways he wanted her made no sense. That he had risked everything—his reputation, his good name—to have her in the first place. That he had betrayed all he stood for, all to taste her as he had.

None of it should have been possible.

But here, in this hotel suite where there was no one to witness his continuing fall from grace— save the wife who had caused it in the first place and who he intended to keep barricaded away from view for years to come—he indulged that ache in him that had ridden him far harder these past six months than he cared to admit.

He did not really kiss her. He plundered her mouth like a man possessed and it was as if all the walls he'd built since that night in the garden came crashing down at once.

Maybe he'd known this would happen. Maybe that was why he'd kissed her only in passing at their wedding ceremony and kept his distance since.

Because once the walls went down, there was nothing between them save the sheer madness of the way he desired her.

Ago remembered this feeling. It had been exactly the same that night in Cornwall, when she'd thrown herself into his arms and kissed him herself, making it clear with her very charming ineptitude that she wanted him with all her sweet innocence. And he'd been kissing her before he meant to and then, despite himself and all his lofty ideals, he had been lost.

Some part of him had been lost ever since.

But tonight was different, he told himself, because she was his wife.

And surely he was owed a wedding night.

He wrenched his mouth from hers and was pleased to find her eyes wide and glazed over with the same passion he felt storming around inside him. He stooped slightly to hoist her up into his arms, only idly noting that she was heavier than she'd been in the garden, as well she should be.

And instead of slowing him down, that she carried his child—his heir, his son—only made the need in him beat harder.

Victoria's lips parted as if she meant to speak, but no words came forth and he found himself grinning as if he'd won some kind of victory. He held her high against his chest and bore her from the room, making his way through the sprawling suite until he found what he was looking for.

A high, well-appointed bed in a chamber that was entirely arranged around the four-poster behemoth at its center, with windows that let the hum of the Eternal City in and a fireplace at the far end to block it out.

He set her down the bed and then turned to build up the fire to keep her warm, happy to discover that unlike those in his family's old villa, this one turned on with a mere switch. That meant he could return to her all the faster.

Back at her side, and following an urge he did not choose to dig into too deeply, Ago went to his knees before her. Beautiful Victoria, with her hair like gold and her eyes like a summer sky, who was looking at him the way she had that night in the garden. As if he was magical, when he had never been anything but dedicated to his own pragmatism. He moved between her legs and then knelt up so he could begin to unbutton the silk shirt she wore, opening it as he went so that he could marvel at her breasts.

When he'd seen them last, they had been pert and high, a pleasure on her lithe frame. Now they were round and heavy and he found himself growling out his approval, opening the clasp between them and baring them to his sight.

Victoria let out a soft sigh and Ago leaned closer, testing the new weight of her breasts in his hands and then leaning closer to sample what he'd uncovered.

And all this time, he'd been tempted to imagine that he'd simply embellished what had passed between them. For surely no woman alive could be this responsive. No woman could be so overcome by his faintest touch that she should toss her head back the way Victoria did, goose bumps breaking out all over her body, her back arching into a bow.

She had done the same thing on a garden bench months ago, tempting him to imagine her innocence was a ruse—but he had been able to taste it. And here, now, everything seem swifter, deeper.

Better than before, when he could admit—at last and only to himself—that he had never imagined anything *could* be better than the passion that had walloped him in the garden last summer.

He could not seem to help himself or hold himself back. Ago sucked one nipple deep into his mouth and felt the way she moaned move through him like a caress. He kept the pressure on one nipple as he found the other, then rolled it gently between his thumb and forefinger. He kept sucking all the while, creating a rhythm between the two that made her wail.

And then, as if he'd conjured her straight from his fantasies, she broke apart and began to shake out her pleasure from that alone.

He kissed his way down her belly, savoring its roundness and finding something primitive inside himself as he did it. As if he was worshiping her, this fertility goddess who had taken his seed and was growing his son. As if he was claiming her. When he would have said that he was far too sophisticated and urbane to ever feel something so…decidedly primal.

By the time he made his way over the mound of her belly, there was nothing sophisticated left inside him. He was all man, all need, and there was no room in him for thoughts of duties or legacies.

There was only one thing he wanted.

Ago tipped Victoria back on the bed and made short work of the flowing skirt she wore. He pushed it up and out of his way, then spread her legs before him so he could inhale, deeply, the scent of her arousal.

He growled in pleasure. Then he wasted no time in tearing the flimsy bit of lace she wore from between her legs, and, at last, bending his head to the scalding, sweet core of her desire.

Where he indulged himself, and drank deep.

And found that here, too, she was far more sensitive than she had been.

He had her writhing within seconds and screaming out his name shortly thereafter.

And so Ago entertained himself, because this was his wedding night and he did not intend to have another. He saw how many times he could build her up to the crest, then throw her over the side. He tested her sensitivity, reveling in it and pushing it, until she was gasping, sobbing, and calling out his name in such a way that he could not tell if she meant to bless or curse him.

He was happy enough with either. Made wild with it, in point of fact.

And it was only when he could take no more, when he had reached an edge inside himself he had never encountered before, that he pulled away. He stood, then shifted her on the bed so that her hips rested on the mattress and he could line himself up between her legs. He grabbed one of the pillows and put it beneath her bottom, raising her up to give him better access, and to make certain he was not tempted to lose himself in what he was doing and crush into her belly.

He worked at his trousers with a certain ferocity, as if he was not certain, even now, that he could contain himself long enough to get where he wished to go—

As if he was some randy adolescent. A stranger to his own control.

It was hard not to think of the last time he had brought the head of his sex to her molten core, and teased himself there, for just a moment. Six months ago, though he'd been lost in her, he'd not been too lost. Despite the driving urge inside him to simply toss aside the practice of a lifetime and surge deep inside her, skin to skin, he'd dug out protection and rolled it on.

And yet when he felt it break deep inside her, he had not been surprised. As if it made sense that with this woman who brought out sensations in him that he had never felt before in all his life, the protection he'd always relied on should fail him.

As if this had all been predestined all along.

Tonight there was no need whatsoever to worry about such things. All he needed to concern himself with was the heat of her. That scalding, deliriously inviting heat. And then, as he notched himself in her entrance, the way she groaned out his name and wrapped herself around him as best she could while he slowly, so very slowly, filled her with the hardest part of him.

With nothing between them this time, save the baby they'd made together.

Only to discover, when she broke all around him, that here, too, she was infinitely more sensitive.

Ago found himself laughing. Because never in all his dutiful days, always with staid and quiet women who never made a fuss even in bed, could he have dreamed of a woman like this. A woman like her. Before, it had been as if Victoria were specifically designed to enthrall him. To enchant him. To take everything he was, everything he wanted to be, and reduce him to nothing but this maddening, encompassing passion. This glorious need. The way her internal muscles gripped him, hard and sure. The way her heels dug into him with every thrust.

The way she came apart for him again and again, his writhing, glorious wonder of a woman—right and beautiful and entirely his.

He wanted to last forever. He wanted to lose himself, again and again.

Ago changed the pace, going harder, deeper. He threw her over the cliff one more time, and then, with a roar, let himself go last.

And when it was finished, when he could move again, he hauled her up into the center of the wide bed. Then he crawled across the mattress to lie beside her, not sure his heart was still safely inside his chest. So hard did it hammer at him. So wild did his own blood feel in his veins.

He had not had the opportunity to catch his

breath. All he could seem to do was lie there, outside himself, not at all sure what just happened to him. But Victoria lay beside him, and he could feel the heat of her. He could feel the weight of her body next to his, pressing into the mattress.

And for a long while, it was enough.

Then when he returned to himself, Ago shifted. He propped himself up on one elbow, so he could take stock of the woman beside him.

The woman he had made his wife. The woman who would soon enough be the mother of his child.

Ago tried to muster up his usual outrage that he had been forced into this situation by his own heretofore unknown inability to control himself—an issue he only appeared to have around this one woman.

His woman, that primitive part of him growled.

Victoria was disheveled in the best possible way. Her lips seemed faintly swollen from his and her eyes had fallen shut as if she had been as turned inside out by what had happened here, between them, as he was. Her skirt had settled back over her thighs, but her breasts were still bared to him and so he reached over to explore them. He traced their alluring shape, drawing tighter and tighter circles on each until the peaks grew rigid once more.

Her eyes fluttered open, and she regarded

him with all of that sunny blue. "My body has changed," she said, matter-of-factly. "Quite a bit."

"And somehow, you're more beautiful for it," Ago replied, his voice low.

He had the strangest urge then, to lean closer and run his teeth down the line of her neck because he knew it made her flush. And then whisper in her ear that he would keep her this way, always. Round with his child, one after the next, ripe and hot and his very own goddess.

And she did not speak Italian fluently, so when he did these things, when he said those words, she only shuddered at the sensation of his teeth, flushed as prettily as he could have hoped, and did not argue.

It made the things he whispered seem like a vow.

Ago hardly understood these urges in him, when he had always considered the inevitable creation of his heir but one more duty to be checked off a list.

But that was before Victoria.

And now he needed to ask himself if he really wanted to lock her up, away from the world, because he was concerned about a scandal…or if he was more like his medieval forebears than he cared to admit.

But he shoved all his dark and unwieldy thoughts aside. Because she was flushed and warm, and he was ready again, and this was the wedding night he should have claimed two weeks ago.

He would not fail to claim it—and her—now. And so, once again, he set himself to the delectable task of discovering her.

Ago did not spare an inch of her body this time. That initial, clamoring need had been met, and so this time, he slowed himself down. He stripped all her clothes from her body. And removed his own.

Then he stretched himself out beside her and dedicated himself to using every trick he knew, the better to make her his in every conceivable way.

And finally, when he had her sobbing anew, he helped her turn on her hands and knees, so he could find his way inside her once again.

A position that did not make him feel less primitive.

Victoria braced herself before rocking back to take the full force of his thrusts. And then moaning each and every time he sunk himself deep.

He had never heard a sweeter music in his life.

Ago wrapped her hair in a coil around one hand. He held her head up, then leaned over the length of her back so he could turn her head and find her mouth. So he could be inside her in two ways.

When she came apart, he went with her.

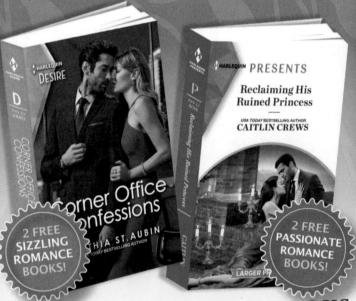

YOU pick your books –
WE pay for everything.
You get up to FOUR New Books and TWO Mystery Gifts...absolutely FREE!

Dear Reader,

I am writing to announce the launch of a huge **FREE BOOKS GIVEAWAY**... and to let you know that YOU are entitled to choose up to FOUR fantastic books that WE pay for.

Try **Harlequin® Desire** books featuring the worlds of the American elite with juicy plot twists, delicious sensuality and intriguing scandal.

Try **Harlequin Presents® Larger-Print** books featuring the glamourous lives of royals and billionaires in a world of exotic locations, where passion knows no bounds.

Or **TRY BOTH!**

In return, we ask just one favor: Would you please participate in our brief Reader Survey? We'd love to hear from you.

This FREE BOOKS GIVEAWAY means that your introductory shipment is completely free, <u>even the shipping</u>! If you decide to continue, you can look forward to curated monthly shipments of brand-new books from your selected series, always at a discount off the cover price! <u>Plus you can cancel any time</u>. Who could pass up a deal like that?

Sincerely

Pam Powers

Pam Powers
For Harlequin Reader Service

Complete the survey below and return it today to receive up to 4 FREE BOOKS and FREE GIFTS guaranteed!

FREE BOOKS GIVEAWAY
Reader Survey

1	2	3
Do you prefer stories with happy endings?	Do you share your favorite books with friends?	Do you often choose to read instead of watching TV?
○ YES ○ NO	○ YES ○ NO	○ YES ○ NO

YES! Please send me my Free Rewards, consisting of **2 Free Books from each series I select** and **Free Mystery Gifts**. I understand that I am under no obligation to buy anything, no purchase necessary see terms and conditions for details.

❑ **Harlequin Desire**® (225/326 HDL GRLR)
❑ **Harlequin Presents**® Larger-Print (176/376 HDL GRLR)
❑ **Try Both** (225/326 & 176/376 HDL GRL3)

FIRST NAME   LAST NAME

ADDRESS

APT.#   CITY

STATE/PROV.   ZIP/POSTAL CODE

EMAIL ❑ Please check this box if you would like to receive newsletters and promotional emails from Harlequin Enterprises ULC and its affiliates. You can unsubscribe anytime.

HD/HP-122-FBG22_HD-HP-122-FBGVR

And Ago had the distinct sensation that though the both of them were lost, they were both found, too. Together.

That was the part that kept him awake.

But that was later. After she'd called down for food and they both ate as if they'd never tasted anything so good before, sitting there before the fire, draped in blankets and quilts to ward off the cold outside. He took her there, too, glutting himself on her when their appetites could no longer be satisfied by.

He'd bathed her, carrying her into the bathroom and using the damp cloth all over her skin with a certain reverence that made his very bones feel loose within his skin.

And then, once more, they'd laid beside each other in the bed, and fanned the flames of that ever-burning fire between them higher. Then higher still.

It was Victoria who crawled over him, testing his sex between her lips the way she had played with his thumb earlier. She kept on until he pulled her away and helped her settle astride him. And then he lay back and let her ride.

At a steady pace until they both came apart.

And now he lay beside her, feeling as if, against his will, not only had all the walls he'd ever built come tumbling down but every veil he'd ever drawn over the darker parts of himself had been ripped aside.

He felt exposed and he did not like it.

Because Ago had learned the lessons his harsh grandfather and bitter father had taught him. And he knew, too well, that there were only two possible roads to take here. And he had already married Victoria, so allowing himself a passionate fling before settling down to his duty was not an option available to him.

Men marry for love when they don't have a legacy, his grandfather had told him once. *Because a legacy requires the kind of love a man might normally bestow upon his wife. Only ask your father what becomes of a man who thinks he can do both.*

They had told him the story a thousand times or more while he was a youth. But he remembered that specific day too well. Because his father had looked at him and for once, had made no attempt to hide the bleakness in his gaze.

I love your mother with all my heart, he had told his son, *and only look what that did to her.*

Ago had been thirteen and well aware of what was expected of him. He had listened to the quiet conversations that went on around him, that had not been for his ears, for years by then.

They had long told him his mother was ill and he had always accepted that. That her illness never got any better was a simple fact, nothing more.

But now he understood why his mother had her own set of nurses. Why he was only permitted to see her under supervision, and why, sometimes, he would hear the mad howling of the wind only to look outside and see that the trees betrayed no hint of any wind at all.

She's mad, he had said that day, and it was a terrible thing, to speak what had only ever been whispered aloud.

She was driven mad, his father had corrected him. *By the weight of responsibilities she was not built for. The fault is mine.*

Boy, choose your wife with your legacy in mind. His grandfather had been frail by then, yet his voice remained strong. *Never let* feelings *set the course of your life. Or you will pay.*

She *will pay*, his father had concluded darkly.

Ago thought that he had taken that in. That he had made it the cornerstone of his existence. It was why he had spent so long selecting potential candidates who he imagined *might* make good wives. His concern had always been living up to his legacy and making sure no stain ever appeared on the family name, or anyone associated with it, as long as he could help it.

His brother notwithstanding.

He had never intended to take for a wife a woman who got under his skin the way Victoria did. He knew she thought that he had considered

her disqualified from consideration because he
was some kind of chauvinist, and he was happy
enough that she think so. It was far better than
the truth.

That being that she was disqualified, eternally,
because she threatened the self-control his entire
life was built upon.

But as he lay in that bed with Rome outside the
windows, Ago found himself smiling.

She set him alight. And Victoria was not experienced. Certainly not experienced enough to
recognize how close to the edge he was whenever
he was near her.

That meant he could use this thing between
them to his advantage.

For Accardis did not divorce. And given how
much he enjoyed her round and pregnant and
bound to him, he saw no reason at all that she
shouldn't remain that way. It was a certainty that
she had not spoken much about *her freedom* as
the night wore on.

He was perilously close to rejoicing.

Because it seemed that for once, Ago could
have everything he wanted. He could do his duty
and sort out the Accardi dynasty. Better yet, he
need not worry that Victoria was not up to the job,
for the truth was, she had been raised to do little
else than carry this kind of weight. She had been
trained to be the wife of a great man, and little as

that might appeal to modern sensibilities, it was what he needed.

That she also happened to have a body that had clearly been created to drive him wild was a bonus.

And not only because the way he wanted her meant he need not find a convenient mistress on the side, as so many men he knew did, thereby becoming the kind of person he had always despised—for *he* did not break vows.

But because it also provided him with an excellent weapon to use against her.

To keep her right where he wanted her. Naked, pregnant, and so out of her mind with desire it would never occur to her to be anything but perfectly compliant.

CHAPTER SEVEN

DECEMBER SPOOLED OUT like a lovely set of twinkly holiday lights, each day a bit brighter than the one before. Christmas was almost upon them. She was married to the father of the baby that grew bigger inside her all the time.

And Victoria still hadn't yet gotten over her shock at how things were turning out between her and Ago after he'd tracked her down in Rome.

She found herself humming her favorite carols to herself as she walked through the villa that morning, smiling as she saw all the holiday cheer.

The Yule log is usually the extent of my family's Christmas decorating, he had told her when she'd asked if there were plans to properly deck the halls.

A log, she had repeated. A bit flatly, it was true.

Sometimes it is also a dessert, he had told her, and since they had been in bed for this conversation, he had leaned in closer to kiss his way down the length of her neck. *Though it is not as sweet as you,* mia mogliettina.

That's not the most festive thing I've ever heard, Ago, she had told him, trying to sound deadly serious while he made her laugh and shiver. *I'm not going to lie.*

Ago had ordered the staff to prepare her a *proper* English Christmas that very same day, and they had gone all out. There were evergreen boughs strewn across every available surface. There were Christmas trees in every room, all decorated and gleaming. And though some might think such distinctly British splendor looked silly against all the Italian grandeur that made the villa such a showpiece, she liked it. It was a little bit of her and Ago, mixed together a lot like the baby they'd made.

The truth was, Victoria kept pinching herself to make sure this new version of her marriage was real. She was afraid she might leave permanent marks and anyway, she wasn't dreaming this.

Because this was not only far better than anything she could have imagined while bracing herself for the sort of marriage her father had intended for her—this was magical.

Ago spent most of his time in Italy with her, flying back and forth to London for specific meetings and occasionally taking her with him when he went further afield. He made it seem as if he was not tending to his empire any longer, but tending to her instead. Mostly by turning her inside out with such consummate skill and wild heat that even thinking about it made her shudder with delight.

The medical team who monitored her from the accommodations Ago had made for them in the villa's converted stables reported that her pregnancy was as healthy as anyone could wish. Between constant confirmation that the baby was well and Christmas cheer everywhere she looked, including lights in the austere column of cypress trees that lined the drive outside, Victoria found that she felt nothing but warmth.

The kind of warmth that had never featured prominently back at home, where her father was about as warm as a block of ice. Especially around the holidays.

But here in Italy, Ago had taught her things she could never have imagined existed. Not just the things that they could do together, naked and inventive. But how it could *feel*. How *she* could feel. Every day was a revelation.

It made her breathless to think she might have missed this.

She paused as she walked down the grand staircase, gazing out the wall of windows that gave her sweeping views over the Tuscan hills. She'd come to love this old, odd villa, slapped together with bits and pieces of all the Accardis who had lived here before her.

Sometimes, in moments like this, she couldn't seem to stop thinking about the fact that all of this had come to her by chance.

What if she had married any one of the men her father had dangled her in front of all these years—as if she had never been anything but bait? What if one of them had bitten? Met her father's ever-escalating price. Taken her and treated her…however it was such men treated the women in their lives. The ones they purchased outright and must therefore view as property. Objects to be used and then cast aside when their usefulness ended or something shinier and newer came along.

Her hope had been to find herself married to a different sort of man, one who would politely see to the making of the necessary heirs and then ignore her thereafter. But either way, once the reality of the marriage had time to settle and become routine and—hopefully—endurable, she'd daydreamed about a lovely little life with room for her to throw herself completely into her charity work and, one day, come over utterly dotty like the best sort of older British woman. She imagined she might raise cats or champion dogs or parakeets, or become a virtuoso gardener renowned the world over for a specific variety of rose.

That had always seemed to her like a happy ending. And yet she knew that there was no possibility that she would feel as she did now.

For she knew full well that there was only one Ago.

Standing there halfway down the stairs, she looked out over the cold, rainy, December morning and smoothed a hand over her bump. "You're going to have a wonderful life, little bit," she murmured to the baby she carried. "Just wait and see. It's already so much better than anyone could have hoped."

Ago had left their bed early this morning, as was his custom. She'd grown used to waking up without him, there in the master suite he'd moved her into when they'd returned from Rome. She'd been so dazzled by him then. So overwhelmed by his brooding masculinity, and all the many ways he could turn her inside out.

She suspected a part of her always would be.

But she was also finding ways to see around the dazzle these days.

That was a good thing. She was starting to get used to the rhythms of this life. A very different life from the one she'd known all these years, forever at her father's beck and call and the focus for all his fury. Instead of having to wake early and attend Everard while he ranted at her about the men he wanted her to meet and the events he wanted her to attend, her mornings here were deliciously lazy. She was grateful that she did not feel a bit off the way she had in the early days of her pregnancy. She'd first thought it was a virus and later had tried her best to ignore how she felt as her fears had mounted.

But here, there was no fear. Here she woke when she liked and took the milky espresso drink provided to her as her single bit of caffeine for the day. Sometimes she nibbled at the biscotti the staff left for her, sometimes not. Then she normally rose and went out for her walk because it turned out that Ago had not misrepresented the many walking opportunities on the estate. She loved all the paths winding in and around the hills, through the vineyards that slumbered at this time of year, and down marvelously romantic lanes lined with more stately cypress trees.

Even in December, Tuscany was beautiful.

Today, however, it was wet. On other mornings she had gone out while it was misting or gray—because she was made of good English stock, thank you, and thrived in a bit of damp—but today the rain was coming down in sheets that reminded her a bit too much of home.

The parts of home she was happy enough to do without.

So instead of heading out, she wandered through the house instead, heading without quite meaning to for the wing she rarely visited. She knew that Ago's office was located in this part of the villa. It was how he ran his empire from afar.

Perhaps today was the perfect opportunity to tell him what she'd dug up in the family library. Old diaries and letters that painted a rather different view of the spotless, dutiful Accardi legacy Ago was always so concerned with. Because she had reason to believe that, in fact, he was descended from regular old human beings with their passions and indiscretions aplenty, just like anyone else.

After these few short weeks together, these long, sweet days and nights that went on forever, Victoria thought he might enjoy getting to know the truth about the relatives he'd kept on so many pedestals for so long. He might welcome the opportunity to look at them face-to-face, for a change.

His business wing was different from the rest of the house. It was newer, clearly installed to feel as much like a modern corporate office as possible in this ancient villa. The walls were bare, with fewer windows—as if the only way for someone to truly work here was to barricade themselves away from all the abundant natural beauty that poured in from everywhere else.

She heard Ago's voice before she saw him and she could conjure him up in her mind to easily, now. He liked to dress for work, even this close to Christmas, and insisted on looking the part on all the video calls he took throughout the day. And the part he played required perfectly tailored suits and innate sophistication, though his natural ferocity fairly hummed in the air all around him.

Maybe it was the contrast that took her breath away.

And Victoria was so busy imagining how handsome he looked, always, that it took her a moment to register what he was actually saying as she drew closer to the room he used as his main office.

Not to mention who he was saying it to.

"I hear you, Everard," he said coolly.

And very distinctly. There was no way she'd misheard him.

Victoria's head spun, out there in the hall. Because she had only ever met one person with that name. It was not a common one. Not like hers.

But she could not accept that Ago was actually speaking to her father.

In the next breath, she told herself she was being silly. Why shouldn't they speak? It was more than likely some or other business thing. Since all these men seemed to do was business. She chastised herself for coming over all silly and emotional. Perhaps it was the pregnancy hormones. In a moment they would start talking figures or contracts or other such boring things, and

she would feel foolish for that strange sensation—
like betrayal—that had flooded her at the sound
of that name.

"I told you those things as a courtesy only,"
she heard her husband say in his cold, measured
way. "Let me assure you, Victoria currently has no
desire to roam anywhere. She's happily pregnant,
happily married, looking forward to Christmas,
and will soon have enough to think about with an
infant in the house. And I doubt very much she
would have found it necessary to sow any wild
oats in the first place if you hadn't treated her
like a medieval virgin princess stuck in a tower
all these years."

Out of the hall, Victoria's heart beat at her,
sickeningly. She had to reach back to steady herself against the wall and was suddenly all too
grateful that this part of the villa was not packed
with the sort of art and statuary that were featured
everywhere else. Because she surely would have
knocked any paintings straight off the walls upon
hearing what sounded like such a casual betrayal
from the husband she'd come to trust.

But then again, why did she trust him? Because
he'd introduced her to the glory of a good orgasm?

You're being paranoid, she told herself sternly.
Maybe a little desperately. And her knuckles
turned white as she gripped the wall on either
side of her, somehow keeping herself upright. *He's*

*never liked your father much, because who could?
No one who's ever met dear Everard has anything
nice to say about him.*

But inside his office, Ago was still speaking.
He let out a bitter sort of laugh that made every
hair on Victoria's body seem to stand on end.

"Do not ask questions you don't want the an-
swers to, Everard," he advised his father-in-law,
his voice dark. "I think you know that I possess
tools you did not. A husband is not the same thing
as a father. And I suspect that is about all you
wish to hear about your daughter's marital bed."

And Victoria tried her best, out there in the
hall, to convince herself that didn't mean…what
it sounded like it meant. But her stomach turned,
because she knew it did. She knew it must. And
everything inside her seemed to be a part of that
same bitter churn. It got more and more precar-
ious, until she found herself hurrying away as
quickly as she could with her ungainly waddle
these days.

She was sick in the powder room near the dining room, but only briefly. So briefly she almost
managed to convince herself that it was a pregnancy thing and unrelated to the fact she'd essen-
tially heard her husband telling her father that he
was controlling her with sex.

Either way, when the nausea passed, Victoria
decided that she would go and walk in the rain

anyway. Because she needed the walk more than she needed to remain dry.

Or in this house a moment more, just now.

Better yet, if her eyes should water as she trekked through the fields, it was as good as not crying at all. Because out in the cold December rain, no one could tell the difference.

Victoria did her best to pretend that she couldn't tell the difference either.

That evening, she dressed for dinner in her overly ripe body. Not as she had before, of course, when it seemed her primary function was to swan about like a clothes hanger for her father's ambitions. She was coming up on eight months pregnant and it was hard to believe that she could get any bigger, though she knew she would. She should have been reveling in the fact she could wear anything that wasn't better suited to be a tent and yet tonight, with a chorus of words from her father hanging all over her like a shroud, she found that she felt more...precarious, somehow, than she ever had before.

She knew that when she made it down into the dining room, Ago would be as he always was. Because for him, nothing had changed.

He, obviously, knew that he'd been manipulating her from the start.

She was the only one who had shattered today, there in an anodyne hallway. She was the only one who felt as if her every breath was being pulled in through broken glass.

Victoria she knew she had to be careful. Because she could march downstairs and confront her husband with what she'd heard. She could take his betrayal and place it squarely on the table where they dined each night and then see what he thought he had to say for himself.

Or she could assume instead that she'd heard all she needed to hear. That despite imagining otherwise, she found herself under the thumb of a man who intended to control her ruthlessly, no matter how she might feel about it.

Maybe the real lesson here was that she should have known better than to hope for anything more.

And at least her father hadn't made any secret of what he was about. He hadn't pretended that he was doing anything at all but keeping her pristine and untouched and as sheltered as possible until it came time to use her for his own ends. That seemed almost refreshing in comparison to Ago, who had taken her innocence, then had taken all that passion he'd taught her and used it against her.

If she could have, she would have walked all the way to Florence today, letting all the sobs inside of her come out as they would. She would have removed herself from this marriage that was exactly like the ones she'd prepared her whole life to endure, when she'd been tricked into imagining it was different. Barring that, she wished she could take this dinner tonight and use it to demand that Ago be honest, for once, about what was happening between them.

But she knew she wouldn't do that. That really, she couldn't, because once again she had to think strategically. It was that or surrender completely. Just…accept that she had been tricked into submission and allow it. Sink into the kind of life she'd always assumed she would lead, and pretend she'd never imagined anything different.

Victoria thought that might actually kill her. Because what horrified her the most, she thought as she smoothed her stretchy dress into place over her belly and headed for the dining room, was that surrender seemed tempting.

It would be so easy, something in her whispered. *You could stop fighting. Surely there are joys enough in this marriage of yours, no matter what his true aims might be. Does it really matter what his intentions are?*

Maybe she was a fool to imagine there should be more. To daydream of a relationship based on honesty, where she didn't have to wonder at every turn if there was a hidden agenda, or purpose that she was deliberately being misled about.

Surely that should be the bare minimum.

Maybe, she thought as she made her slow way down the hall from the master suite, this was her fault. Maybe there was something inherently wrong in her that led every man she met to think that lying to her and manipulating her was necessary. Maybe it served some greater good she couldn't see.

As she walked down the halls of this ancient old house, she tried to make her breath deep and even. And as she did, she found herself looking at the art on the walls, much of it the kind of ambitious works that belonged in museums. But mixed in with the prestige pieces were paintings of the villa itself. Or meditations on the grounds, the hills, the vineyards. And portrait after portrait of figures from the great Accardi past.

She ignored the men with their improbable blue eyes and dark, brutally sensual features. She focused on the women instead, standing in strange positions and surrounded by hostile-looking relatives. And something about their mysterious smiles through history calmed her.

Because surely, the marriage she found herself in was no different than those expected of women since the dawn of time. It was only recently, relatively speaking, that anyone had married for love or even companionship. For most of history, Victoria's situation had been more common. A match arranged by her father, her own wishes ignored. The expectation had always been that she would

make the best of whatever situation she found herself in.

That's what the women who smiled down at
her tonight had done. Generation after generation,
the Accardi wives had been brought to this same
villa and left to figure out how to thrive no matter
what sort of marriage they found themselves in.

Bitter or brutal. Cruel or cold. Even passionate or sweet. They could have had no idea what
awaited them when they arrived here. Victoria
knew all too well that the promises made to a
blushing bride did not necessarily come to anything.

All she really needed to do was find a way to
be all right with being a part of this same sweep
of history.

She felt the full weight of all those centuries
as she made her way into the dining room and
paused in the doorway, her eyes moving over
Ago as he stood at the windows with his back to
her. She wondered what he saw, looking out into
the darkness that came so early this time of year,
knowing that everything for miles in all directions was his.

Victoria included.

She felt a great surge of conviction within her,
but she didn't really know what it was she planned
to do until he turned to face her. She didn't know

herself, not truly, until she smiled wide and guile-less, then moved into his arms.

As if she'd heard nothing today.

As if everything was as it was when she'd woken up this morning.

As if she was still that foolhardy.

Ago kissed her as if he was starving for her taste and she kissed him back with equal fervor, and there was a relief in that. To lose herself in all that slick heat, where it didn't matter what she knew or what he'd said, because there was only that fire. And the only thing that felt real was that mad heat.

Ago pulled back and looked down at her, his gaze brooding, searching.

This morning Victoria would have assumed that he was battling the same overwhelming feel-ings that she was. Tonight, she knew better. He was looking to see if this spell he wove around her had worn off. He was admiring his handiwork.

But she was an Accardi wife, like it or not. She was made of sterner stuff. Victoria smoothed her hands over her belly the way she liked to do, to check in with her baby, and it settled her. She was made of sterner stuff because she had to be. Be-cause she would raise her son to be the best man he could be, despite what his father might try to instill in him.

Because Ago liked his ghosts. That meant Victoria would have to find a way to make sure her child knew the bright light of day.

"You appear to have weighty matters indeed on your mind, *mia mogliettina*," Ago said as he led her to her seat with that offhanded courtliness that might have made her swoon, yesterday.

But today she wondered if even that ingrained courtesy of his was just another weapon he used against her. If it was as false as the rest.

"There's only one weighty matter that occupies my thoughts," she said with the smile he would expect as he drew her chair as close to the table as she could manage, with her belly getting in the way. Victoria found that she was grateful even for that, because for all it made her feel clumsy and unlike herself, she liked the distance her belly provided. Ago had long since dispensed with making her sit down at the foot of the table while he sat at the head. Now they shared a corner. And she had found that so charming. So sweetly intimate.

Tonight she wondered if she might be able to get away with "accidentally" stabbing him with the tines of her fork.

But that was unduly bloodthirsty. And besides, it would give her game away.

"It will not be long now," Ago said as he sat in his usual place. "Soon enough the child will be here and a new generation of this family will begin."

Victoria just kept on smiling as the staff brought in their first course. There was quiet as the platters were placed between them with great ceremony. And then as Ago waited for her to pick up her fork before applying himself to the antipasti. She served herself some of the risotto, but she didn't sample it. Instead, she felt her smile grow sharper at the edges.

"I've been spending my afternoons in the family library," she told him.

"There is not much there," he replied, his attention on the prosciutto and cheese before him. "It is mostly memorabilia. If you are looking for novels of note or volumes to expand your thinking, I would direct you to the main library instead."

"One thing I am not lacking," she said, and it was a greater effort to keep her voice pleasant than she'd expected, "is education, Ago. Thanks to fearsome nuns and terrifying Jesuits. I'm not sure your Cambridge dons could outmatch them."

He laughed at that. "By all means, then. Rot your brain attempting to understand the maudlin scribbles of entirely too many of my ancestors."

"Your grandmother and your great-grandmother kept detailed diaries."

A dark brow arched. "I did not realize you read Italian."

"They are in English. Your great-grandmother

wished to keep her thoughts private from the staff. Your grandmother agreed." She could smell the truffles in the risotto and she already knew that the cook was an artist, but still, she couldn't taste a thing. "Your great-grandmother was called Isadora and it seems that your great-grandfather got her as a kind of barter."

Ago placed his fork on his plate with extraordinary precision. Then he lifted his eyes and gazed at her in that arrogant amazement of his. "I beg your pardon?"

Victoria did her best to ignore the sudden chill. "Her father was at one time a very rich man, by all accounts. But he fell into difficulties after the first World War, which is perhaps unsurprising. He became a bit reckless, Isadora reckoned, as men of his station were wont to do. Having so little experience with any consequences of note." Ago continued to stare at her in that astonished way that made her feel like a pauper who'd insulted a prince. She had to remind herself that there was no royalty here. And no paupers either. "Your great-grandfather was smitten. He did not require a dowry and better still, paid off the bulk of his father-in-law's debts, all so he could marry Isadora."

"I was always told that she was a rare beauty,"

Ago said. "She was said to have bewitched the better part of Europe in her day."

"If by that you mean she took a great many lovers, yes," Victoria said. Serenely.

Her husband's dark gaze swung to hers. "I am certain you are mistaken."

"Not according to her diary," Victoria replied. "She considered herself quite an accomplished lover, in fact. She and your great-grandfather took great pleasure in choosing lovers for one another, and then playing them off each other."

She could admit that the stunned silence that followed that pronouncement was pleasant.

So pleasant that it seemed to return her appetite to her. She dug into her risotto with gusto, and when the staff swept back in with the usual *secondi* and *contorni* dishes, cooked meats and plates of vegetables to tempt any palate or mood, she heaped her plate high.

Ago did not speak until they were alone again. "Are you suggesting... Do you *dare* to suggest that my great-grandparents were...*swingers*, Victoria? Are you unwell?"

"I'm not suggesting it," Victoria said merrily, as if she hadn't heard his frigid tones. "I'm telling you that they were. And they were quite happy. What they were not, as far as I can tell, was at all

concerned that their hobbies would impact nega-
tively on the family name."

She felt more than saw Ago's frown, then. In
all its ferocity.

But she was only getting started.

"Your grandparents were far more conven-
tional, mind you," she continued, applying herself
to her meal as if she was unaware that he was having an intense reaction to her words. An intense
negative reaction, that was. "Your grandmother's
family was well known to yours, it seems. Your
grandmother wrote that she and your grandfather
were raised together, for all intents and purposes.
She had known your grandfather her whole life
by the time he asked her to marry him."

Ago had stopped pretending he was eating. He
now stared at her, as if attempting to stop her from
continuing on by the force of his brutal regard
alone. Victoria had the full force of his attention,
God help her, and that was what mattered.

She reminded herself that this was what she
wanted. To be a player in her own life, for once.
Even if it was only for the length of this meal, it
was something.

And *something* had to be better than the whole
lot of nothing she'd always known.

"If I were you, I'd be very careful, *mia mogliettina*." His voice was far darker, far colder, than

the December night outside. "My grandfather was one of the finest men I have known."

"I'm sure that he was," Victoria replied with tremendous calm. She felt none of it, but she could sound as if she did. That, too, felt like something. "But you see, by her reckoning, he knew that your grandmother loved another. He convinced her that because they had grown up together, they could marry as friends. They could be merry companions who wanted the same things out of a life."

"My grandfather was not a clown. He was not *merry*. He was a great man, revered by all who knew him. And he is responsible for taking Accardi Industries out of the bucolic hills of Tuscany and into the global market."

"She suspected that he was desperately in love with her," Victoria continued, as if sharing secrets with a close friend. "But he promised her that wouldn't matter. The problem is that such promises are made to be broken, aren't they? He resented that she could not love him. She suspected that he built up the business not only to impress her, but to prove to her that she was a hundred times a fool to have given her heart to some low-class carpenter who could never provide for her as he did." She smiled at her husband. "Then they were trapped, both of them desperately and hopelessly in love with someone they could not have.

As far as I can tell from the diaries they both left behind, neither one of them was ever untrue. But your grandmother turned to drink. Your grandfather became embittered. They were held up as great paragons of virtue to all who knew them, but the truth is that they were excruciatingly unhappy."

Ago looked as if he wanted to bolt up from his seat, though he did not. She watched, telling herself she felt nothing as that muscle in his jaw worked. Telling herself she was happy that she had brought these things to his attention, dropping them like bombs over dinner.

She had intended to tell him all this earlier today, after all. Though she would not have presented the facts quite so baldly, she could admit.

Still, she was glad she had. He needed to know. She assured herself that was not her bravado talking, despite the flush she could feel in her cheeks that suggested otherwise.

"Do you take some pleasure in digging up these graves?" Ago looked at her as if she had done something to him. As if the facts she had recited here were an assault. Victoria wanted to explain herself. She felt the urge race through her—but she bit her tongue. "And have done so, with such obvious relish, do you truly imagine that I would wish to hear such unsavory details? I remember my grandparents, Victoria. They might not have loved each other, but then, that was not the purpose of their marriage. The purpose was doing their duty, and they did their jobs. They did them well."

"What I'm trying to suggest to you, husband, is that you can choose how you do this duty of yours, to which you have dedicated the whole of your life. Your great-grandparents were of a like mind. And happy for it. Your grandparents were miserable. Nothing you have ever told me, or I have heard, about your parents suggests that *they* were anything but—"

"Devoted," Ago bit out, his dark eyes a blaze of warning.

And the truth was, she was just as happy not to touch on the issue of his parents.

"This is what it suggests to me," she said instead, telling herself that she disliked him as she set her gaze to his, though the lick of flame that worked through her whispered that she was a liar. "That even you, such a lifelong devoted servant to the Accardi legacy, can choose the path that suits you. If you wish. That's all." Victoria shrugged, but perhaps a bit too elaborately, because his eyes narrowed. "Because they were all just people. Not giants or celestial beings who you feel so compelled to live up to. Just regular people. Nothing more, nothing less. Some of them were virtuous, others not. I suspect the real truth is that they were all bits of both. As are we all."

He did not move. He did not seem to so much as breathe, but then, Victoria found she could not draw in any air herself. It was as if he caged her with his arms, locking her down into her seat. When in reality he was still seated at the head of the table, his eyes blazing, not a finger on her. No cage at all.

Save that of her own making.

"Is this something you would like to confess?" he asked, his voice cold. "Have these pleasures we have discovered together so enchanted you that you have decided you must experiment with them? To traipse about the continent, taking lovers? Because I must warn you, Victoria. It doesn't matter what you've read. I am not a man who shares what is his. Ever."

And deep inside her, something seemed to sing to her at that. Even though there was a wild, reckless part of her that wanted to rush to her feet and announce that she intended to follow in his great-grandparents' footsteps and cut a swathe through the male population. *Don't worry*, she could tell him, with great sophistication and a hint of boredom, as she imagined the sort of women who wanted such lives always spoke. *I'll be cer-*

tain to keep you informed of my each and every move. In detail.

But she knew she only wished to say such things to him to see if she could poke him into displaying that emotion that she knew—she *hoped*—lurked just beneath his skin. Locked away long ago by this idea of his that every breath he took had to be dutiful, or he didn't deserve to take it.

This isn't supposed to be about him at all, something in her argued. *This is supposed to be about* you, *claiming some measure of revenge here. Making him regret his manipulations however you can.*

Either way, Victoria wanted to push him. She wanted to make him fall apart, the way she had, by any means necessary. But instead, she only smiled, and shook her head.

"Of course not," she said, though she hadn't given a great deal of thought to indiscriminate sex. Maybe it was because she'd fallen pregnant after having sex exactly once. It seemed to have put a damper on any notion that she ought to go freewheeling about, notching up bedposts. "I only thought that as we will soon have our own son to raise, we might concentrate less on duty, as it can be interpreted in so many ways. And more on being a good man. A decent human. A person who would never lie or deceive another. Just a thought."

But he did not seem to follow her where she was going, straight back to himself and their marriage.

"You say duty like this a bad thing," Ago replied in a low, taut voice, his gaze so dark it hurt to look at him directly. Though Victoria did it anyway. "While I have always considered it a guiding light. And if there is any gift I could give my son, it would be that. Because it would always lead him home."

And later, in their bed, she could feel the intensity come off of Ago in waves. She could *feel* the emotion in him—

But he never broke.

He gave in to his passion, eventually, but no matter how she tried to do to him what he did to her, to make him beg her as he fell apart in her hands, he never let her.

And so she curled up on her side and pretended to be asleep, his heavy arm slung over her body, his hand on the bump where their son slept. While all the while, inside, she told herself that she could deal with *her* feelings much better than he could, and so she would.

She could start by remembering that he had set out to control her by this deception, this pretense that he was as besotted with her as she was with him.

He had led her to believe that what burned between them meant something.

But the only fire in him was for his bloody name.

Victoria needed to remember that. She needed to know it in her bones. So she could work on leaving him, once and for all.

CHAPTER EIGHT

Ago did not have particularly fond recollections of Christmas. Like most things in his family, there were usually command performance appearances, duties to acquit and responsibilities to meet.

The traditional meatless dinner on Christmas Eve, a pageant of seafood that his family had always made longer and more trying by filling the table with local dignitaries and the odd overawed peasant—the better to extol the virtues of the restrained and elegant Tuscan character while feasting. Christmas Day had meant the local church, endless masses, and then stilted formal meals that had been tedious and awkward until he'd come of age and could retreat into the good whiskey like everyone else.

But that wasn't the end of it, for the 26th was *il giorno di Santo Stefano*, when his family would ostentatiously parade from one nativity scene in a local church to the next, giving donations to all, then hitting up the hospitals for more opportunities to display their benevolence. Only to return to the villa for yet another too-long meal, which usually devolved into recriminations and histrionics that everyone pretended not to remember for the rest of the Christmas season, which in Italy stretched on until the Epiphany in January. There would be visits from La Befana, the *strega* from folklore who delivered stockings filled with sweets in the night, and yet another family meal during the day—a national holiday—during which his mother and grandmother would murmur things like *L'Epifania, tutte le feste porta via* to each other and into their wine, as if the Epiphany not only took the holidays away for the year but all of their hope and happiness too.

Buon Natale, one and all.

But despite his aversion to the spectacle, Ago had made an effort this year. He had told himself it was all part and parcel of giving Victoria what she wanted, and thus to continue lulling her into a false sense of security. Because it was clear to him that Victoria, having lost her mother at a young age, was certain to throw herself full tilt into the mothering of their child.

He knew this by the way she crooned to her bump when she thought she was alone. The way she talked to their child on their walks, pointing out items of interest as if the baby inside her could see what she saw.

No matter how much help she might have on hand, as befit the mother of his heir, he was certain that she would insist on being as hands-on as possible. Unlike his grandmother, who been far more concerned with appearances and what she thought was owed to the community as the reigning Accardi matriarch. Or his mother, who had been distant and medicated and under constant supervision on the few occasions per year she actually interacted with her sons.

Your mother had a responsibility to produce the two of you, his father had said whenever Ago or Tiziano dared complain. *Whatever you may think of her, she did her duty. You can do her the simple courtesy of appreciating what she did without forever expecting more. Can you not?*

Ago had done exactly that. He had expected nothing from his mother after the age of nine or so, up until her death when he was fourteen. And by the time his father had died when he was twenty-one, he'd stopped expecting anything from that quarter too. And in the meantime, he'd learned a great many valuable lessons about the ways it was possible to arrange events to suit himself without seeming to do so.

It was only one of the ways he was good at his job.

With Victoria, it had seemed the easiest thing imaginable to play the besotted newlywed. It had not been difficult to do his best to keep her lost in a haze of sensual bliss until the child arrived. After all, there were only a few months left. Why not make sure this marriage he hadn't wanted ran as smoothly as possible, so that his son and heir could have a lovely and joyful start?

He wasn't sure that he'd enjoyed anything like that upon his arrival into this family, if he parsed the stories he'd been told about his childhood.

Not that Ago liked to do much parsing.

Besides, it was easy enough to run his office from the villa. His grandfather had built this wing for precisely that purpose. His father had used it more often than not, particularly during the years Ago's mother was the most unwell. Ago's own staff were well used to him going mobile, since he routinely traveled to the various Accardi Industries offices around the world. He'd even taken Victoria with him on some of those more recent jaunts, though he had not paraded her about as his wife.

He had seen to it that the fact that they had married was mentioned nowhere. He couldn't control whispers, but he could do his best to sink stories before whispers became questions he might need to answer for his stockholders.

Because what he was doing—what all of this

was, as he reminded himself daily—was sticking to his plan.

Even if the trappings were a bit different than he might have originally intended.

The idea of using the Christmas season to help keep her docile had occurred to him late. He had walked with her one morning here, through the cold mists that snaked over the hills and gathered in the valleys. And he had become so accomplished at playing his part that he found himself taking her hand without even thinking that he ought to do it. Rubbing his thumb over the back of hers, he'd swung their arms slightly as they moved together at a pace that seemed to come to them both naturally.

If it was real, he might have thought they were uniquely suited to each other.

It is so beautiful here, Victoria had said, her clear blue eyes fixed off into the distance. *It will be lovely to have our first Christmas here.*

What do you normally do for Christmas? he had asked in some astonishment, for it had not occurred to him until that moment that Christmas was something she would expect to celebrate. Or even what it might mean to her, if it meant anything at all.

When, really, he should have done. As far as he had ever been able to tell, the moment it began to get dark in the afternoons in England the whole country went Christmas mad. By early December, it was nearly impossible to find an Englishman who was capable of conducting a serious business meeting, too busy were they all with their holiday merrymaking and their ugly sweaters and their fancy dress parties.

The Italian preference for a Christmas season that ran for roughly a month, from the 8th of December through to the Epiphany, seemed very nearly rushed in comparison.

My father was not one to celebrate the holiday, Victoria had told him. *By his reckoning, the gifts he gives all year round, for which I ought to be more grateful, are more than enough. Still, I take pleasure in all the decorations. I like all those lights, sparkling so happily even though the nights are long.*

Ago had smiled down at her she gazed up at him. *How am I to know how to give you the Christmas you desire if you don't tell me?*

She had laughed at that, and though he'd only said that because it seemed like the right thing to say, he had suddenly been determined that he would, by God, deliver her the perfect Christmas.

He'd told himself it was simply another way to sweeten the pot.

I don't actually want anything particularly special, she'd said, still laughing, the sound somehow making the mist all around them feel bright. *Ever-*

greens and candles. Christmas carols. Something festive and happy and with no talk of gratitude owed, that's all.

Ago had set his staff to the task of researching the quintessential British Christmas and then making it happen, right here in the villa. Both the things she already knew of and the things he'd kept in reserve.

He had thought that they'd nailed it. Victoria had seemed delighted at first. Her lovely face had gone soft when she'd caught sight of the Christmas trees that shed their needles in every room. Her eyes had glowed when she'd seen the fairy lights strewn on the branches of everything that stood through the winter outside, from trellises to trees.

But over the past few days he had the sense that he was missing something, somehow. And he was not used to missing things. He was Ago Accardi. He made millions without even thinking about it, all thanks to his discernment.

Yet Victoria grew more opaque by the day.

He'd tried to put his finger on what could have happened, but it had proved impossible. There had been that night when she'd laid out all those things he did not wish to know about his great-grandparents and his grandparents, but he hadn't argued about it any further. Mostly because what she'd said made a great many parts of his childhood suddenly make a lot more sense. Perhaps more sense than he might have wished.

And he didn't think she'd intended to wound him with her discoveries, because she'd come to him with all of her typical generosity and greed in bed that night. And every night thereafter.

Ago knew all kinds of women who could hold hatred in their hearts and still enjoy the marital bed. Apparently, some of his forebears were among them. But he could not believe that Victoria was that jaded.

Not yet.

And still, he found her more difficult to read by the day. Maybe because of that, he found himself returning to the things she'd said over and over. He'd even found those diaries himself, when he'd never had the slightest inclination to delve into what his family members, all long dead, had got up to behind closed doors.

But if what Victoria had said was true—and he discovered, sadly, that it was not only true, but that his great-grandmother had a flair for the descriptive—it meant that everything his grandfather and father had beaten into him since he was small was...

Not quite right. Not right and more, not even a fair representation of their own lives.

Particularly when he considered his own parents and what he'd observed of their relationship—yet had decided was none of his concern.

It was possible his father had encouraged him to think it none of his concern, now he considered it.

But he did not wish to dwell on any of that. No matter how many times it seemed to appear in his head despite his wishes.

Ago woke Christmas morning feeling…unlike himself.

He reached out for Victoria, but found her side of the bed cold. He sat up, adrenaline spiking inside him, but saw that she had only taken herself over to the seating area before the fireplace. She sat in the chair she favored with her legs drawn up, wrapped in several throws, with an expression on her face that he could not recognize as she gazed into the dancing flames.

And he could not have said why it was that he found himself rubbing his hand over his chest, as if he could rub away the sense of disquiet that moved in him.

"Is this the Christmas spirit of which I've heard so much?" he asked into the quiet hush of the room.

Victoria turned her head to look at him, smiling widely. Guilelessly, he thought. Ago told himself he must have been imagining that wistful look.

It must have been something else he didn't quite recognize, that only reminded him of despair.

"Come," he said gruffly, discomfited by the train of his thoughts. "I have something to show you."

And he found himself watching her too closely as she rose, then came to the foot of the bed, as if she was made entirely of obedience and desire. Something he should have celebrated, surely. Instead, it made him feel entirely too close to unnerved.

He studied her the way he did too often these last days, looking for signs. Looking for hints. Looking for *something*. She was wearing one of the nightgowns she favored that stretched over her belly and made her look like some kind of confection, all the sweet cream of her flesh with that rich, brown fabric stretched over her like so much chocolate.

As ever, he wanted to eat her up.

But it was Christmas and he felt…too many things. And he disliked all of them, but there seemed only one way to handle things. *Christmas first*, he told himself darkly.

He rolled from the bed and threw on the silk trousers he wore to keep from horrifying his staff. And also to attempt to tamp down on the endless longing he felt for this wife of his.

It never mattered how many times he took her

in the night. He always wanted more. That was why he always left her in the bed when he started his day, because she was more heavily pregnant by the day and delicate, no matter what she might think. But now they were standing close together, with so little in the way of clothes between them. So close that he wasn't sure which one of them was breathing, because it seemed as if they shared the same breath—

But thinking about tumbling her down to the bed right now wasn't exactly what he had in mind as a Christmas gift.

That could come later. He was sure it would.

And Ago was no good at gift giving. He wasn't sure he'd ever actually...given anyone a gift, in fact. Not one that meant anything to him. Or, hopefully, to the recipient.

He stepped back, perhaps a bit abruptly. Victoria gazed back at him, looking slightly baffled, and he couldn't blame her. He rubbed at his chest again, and then he took her arm.

Formally, as if they were entering a ballroom.

Instead, he guided her in her nightgown through the connecting door that had once separated the master's bedroom from the mistress's, that they might share or not share their bedchambers as it suited them. He had told Victoria it was used for storage and kept it locked.

"Am I being relegated to a separate bedroom?"

she asked, and he told himself that edge in her voice was amusement, nothing more. "So soon?"

Ago said nothing. He told himself it was because there was no need to look for ghosts in everything, even the way she spoke to him.

But that persistent ache in his chest suggested otherwise.

He did not allow himself to rub at it again. Instead, he watched as Victoria took in the room. He braced himself as she let out a small noise.

She let go of his hand and moved further into the room, turning she could see what he'd had the staff working on, stealthily, for some time.

"A nursery," Victoria breathed, as if she couldn't quite make sense of it. Though he did not know what else a room like this could be, outfitted with a crib, a changing table, a rocking chair, and a cozy little sofa. A bright rug on the floor and happy pictures on the pale yellow walls. "You made me a nursery?"

"I think you know, *mia mogliettina*, that I did no such thing with my own two hands," Ago said stiffly. "I took an advisory position in this."

He didn't know what was wrong with him. Why his limbs felt awkward and ungainly when he worked hard to ensure he was neither, ever. Why he could not seem to look at her directly, nor look away, when he prided himself on his directness in all things.

"It looks…" Victoria turned in a full circle, hugging herself. When she turned back to face him, her eyes were shining. "Ago. It looks exactly like my nursery. The one in my father's house, only with Tuscany outside the windows instead of England."

"I insisted that your father send me photographs," Ago said, as if it hurt to get the words out. He found that, in fact, it did. "I thought you would like it."

She looked as if she was having trouble swallowing. "I do. I really do."

And then they stood there, staring at each other, and Ago—who had never felt himself unequal to anything—found himself as close to floundering as he had ever been.

He didn't know if it was Christmas that was getting to him. The fact that he was celebrating it, apparently. More likely it was the fact that he had given her a gift like this—a gift that was not the sort of thing he could accomplish with a mere wave of his hand while he concentrated on other things. This nursery had actually required thought.

Ago told himself that he did this only to sweeten the pot. To make her happy to stay put, right where he wanted her. That it was simply a gesture, nothing more, and had nothing to do with *him*.

Though now, looking at her, he understood that he really hadn't thought this through.

Because now he felt that he'd revealed more of himself than he'd intended to, and worse, he was clearly exposing himself in a way he would have avoided entirely, had he realized this was how it would go.

It felt like a misfire, if he was honest.

And he was Ago Accardi, so he had no experience with such things.

He still couldn't read the look on Victoria's face. She looked almost solemn as she reached out and took his hands. Then she brought them to her belly and smoothed them into place, leaving them there.

As if this was her gift.

And the strangest thing was that it felt like one.

It was not as if he hadn't touched her belly before. There was no part of her he had not touched. But at the same time, Ago had not touched her belly quite like *this*. He had not…lingered.

He certainly had not done what he did now, leaning down so he could press his lips to the crest of her belly, and in no particular hurry.

Ago heard her breath leave her raggedly. But all he could focus on was the heat of her, seeming to blaze through the fabric of her nightgown. That was another gift, surely, because he could feel that heat wrap around him and pour into him.

But better yet was his own son, there within her, who kicked as if he already knew his father.

God willing, a better father than his own had been.

A sentiment so unusual, and so forbidden, that Ago could hardly believe he'd admitted to feeling such a thing.

Maybe that was why he found himself on his knees, where he could press his kisses all over her belly and, for once, not because he intended to build that wildfire between them. For once, simply, because she was his and she was carrying his baby.

Because this was his wife and his son.

Because like it or not, plan or no plan, this was his family.

And that word seemed to land in him differently, today.

He looked up to find her watching him, her blue eyes wide, tears making trails down her cheeks.

"Buon Natale," he told her, though his voice was gruff. "Merry Christmas, *mia mogliettina*, and you too, my son."

When she made a broken little noise, he helped her down to kneel with him. Then he kissed her mouth, again and again, until it was better. Until she was sighing, not sobbing.

And soon enough the strange mess of feelings

gave way to lust and longing, and other such comprehensible things.

It was a relief to help her move astride him, there on the floor of their first child's nursery on a Christmas morning that seemed swollen with portent.

Ago told himself that this had been his aim all along.

Sex. Passion. Nothing more, nothing less.

Those things that had ruined him in her uncle's garden that he could use, here, to bind her to him so tightly that she would never think to leave. That she would never think to care that he had made her choose her own cage, after all.

Better still, that she would never notice that despite his best intentions, he'd made a critical error.

And had somehow ended up on the wrong side of the bars with her.

CHAPTER NINE

VICTORIA HAD NOT been prepared for the nursery.

Later that night, replete on the proper British Christmas dinner that the Italian cook had attempted to put together, complete with crackers at every plate and all the plum pudding she could eat, Victoria stood in the middle of the nursery floor. She hugged the drapey sweater she wore tighter around her, wondering why this was all so much more difficult than she'd expected.

The moon was high, coursing into the windows and making it far too easy to imagine what it would be like if she simply…stayed here. Just a few months from now she could sit right there in that rocking chair, holding her baby while he nursed. It would be easy. A blink of the eye between now and then. And here, in this room that made her feel so at home—in a way she hadn't felt since she was a child and didn't know the sorts of things her father had planned for her as she grew—she could be happy.

She knew she could. She might even convince herself that she was loved.

For what else could send a man like Ago on a quest to perfectly replicate the look of a room he shouldn't have known existed? What could possibly have possessed him?

And thinking of it that way, she could even put what she'd overheard into context. Maybe he didn't feel the way she'd assumed he must, outside his office, clinging to that bare, white wall. Maybe he didn't think that he was trying to manipulate her at all. Maybe he'd said the kinds of things he had because he was trying to play to her father's prejudices.

But standing there, drenched in moonlight, she blew out a breath and laughed.

Bitterly, and a little too long.

Because Victoria knew this particular cycle too well. She'd spent most of her life telling herself stories just like this to explain how her father treated her.

And what she knew was that stories were comforting. Stories were like light in the dark. Good stories could excuse away even the most egregious behavior.

But that didn't make them true.

She turned and snuck back through the connecting door into the bedchamber she'd shared with Ago for nearly a month now. Already, it was hard to imagine sleeping on her own again. When before, she would have said that it was unimaginable that she could ever actually figure out how to sleep with another person beside her. Much less a man like him, so big, so implacably male.

Victoria would have sooner curled up with a lion.

He slept even now, the moon playing over the planes and angles of his beautiful body as he lay there.

She really didn't know why it was she'd lingered here.

What she truly this sad? That one lovely Christmas, and one admittedly thoughtful gift, should make her question her own convictions?

Inside, her baby kicked. Hard enough to make her wince. And for no reason at all, she felt tears well up, sudden and fierce, tipping over to track their way down her cheeks.

"I know," she whispered, so low that it was hardly more than her own heartbeat. "I love him too."

And that seemed to dance there in the moonlight that teased its way into the room and made Ago look even more beautiful than he was. *I love him*, Victoria thought, and the wonder of that almost brought her to her knees.

But reality chased in behind it, keeping her on her feet.

The baby kicked again, and she felt the kick of a headache. She tried to blink it away. "But we deserve more than a cage, little bit," she murmured. "No matter how pretty it is."

And then she made herself turn, though it hurt. And even as she headed for the door, she knew she was committing every detail of the scene before her to memory. The way Ago's dark lashes looked, there against the arrestingly masculine planes of his beautiful face. How easy he looked in repose, when he was always so stern and commanding awake. Sleeping, he could have been a different man. A softer, more approachable one.

But that was just another story to tell herself. To make the way she felt about him okay, when she knew it was probably just a little Stockholm syndrome mixed in with the Christmas pud.

Victoria tiptoed out of the bedchamber, and this time, she didn't let the lure of the nursery call her back. She made herself walk as quietly and as quickly as she could through the rest of the master suite, then out into the hall.

She was tracing his back in her mind, thinking of all the times she'd explored it with her mouth, her hands. She was thinking of the hard grip of his hands and how they held her hips where he wanted them when she rode him, swift and so sweet.

But if it was only sex, she was sure it would be easier to leave.

Not that she really had the slightest idea what *only sex* meant, really, given that this was all the sex she'd ever had. But that was what people said, wasn't it? *Only sex*, as if coming together the way she and Ago had wasn't life altering. When his touch could transport her so easily and there was a part of her that feared that it didn't matter whether she left him or not.

In some way, she knew, she would always be held tight in the palm of his hand.

"That's only a story," she told herself as she waddled along. "And not a very nice one."

Her headache bloomed a bit brighter, but she kept moving through the house despite the pain. It was dark and quiet now, no carols playing softly. Instead, she could smell all the pine trees and the wax of the candles that burned in the windows. It was like creeping through a Christmas card, and she didn't know whether she should find that a bit creepy or so sweet it might make her cry.

Instead of succumbing to all the tugging on her heartstrings, she thought about what she would do now. She wouldn't stay in Italy this time. That was just asking for trouble, and if Rome had proved anything to her, it was that she couldn't be trusted not to crumble at the first sign of adversity. And luckily, no one knew she was married to Ago. No one would be on the lookout for a hugely pregnant British woman, thinking they could use her against him.

She would be safe as houses and also the size of a house, and that thought made her giggle a little, even through the headache.

The baby moved again, and she had to stop then. Because there was an ache inside, first sharp, then dull, and it didn't feel like the usual game of football with her internal organs. She held on to the nearest wall, ignored the Picasso, and breathed a bit more. Until, eventually, the clench of pain eased a little.

"Come on, baby boy," she muttered. "We have to be a team on this."

And this time, as she passed all the portraits of the Accardi ancestresses, she felt as if they were judging her. Because *they* hadn't left.

Even, perhaps, when they should have.

But was that what she wanted for herself? Was Victoria really required to martyr herself to the legacy of this place, this family, just because her husband saw no other way to live? More importantly, was that the life she wanted for her son?

Or maybe the real truth, she admitted as she heaved herself down the stairs, was that she wanted the life on offer here far too much. Because she might not have been able to go out and find work, the way others her age did. Her father would never have allowed that. But she had spent her life engaged in charity work instead, because that was what was open to her. And she had loved it.

And so she knew that a legacy shared was less like a curse and more like something magic, made better because it drew those who carried it closer together. Or it could be.

But Ago didn't want that.

She might love him, but he didn't love her.

He wanted only to convince her that more was happening here than it was. He wanted her to lose herself in this, in him. He wanted to make her so dizzy and deliriously in love with him that it wouldn't occur to her to do anything but obey him.

He was just like her father. And in many ways he was much more insidious.

Because her father wasn't playing any games. She doubted he was capable of that kind of subterfuge. Her father hadn't pretended she was anything but a pawn since she'd hit puberty and it had been clear she was the kind of pretty that he could leverage.

Meanwhile, Ago had been playing her for a fool since Rome.

And that was the part she couldn't forgive.

The main stair in the villa was long and dramatic. And tonight it was lit up so brightly by the

moon outside that she felt as if all the paparazzi
that Ago had been avoiding all this time had found
her at last and were blinding her on purpose. No
wonder her headache wouldn't quit.

It was one more indication that she absolutely
should not stay here. Because she already felt
weak and ashamed and like she would really prefer to just turn around and hurry herself right
back into bed.

Who knew what he could make her do if she
stayed here, and let him play the role of doting
father? She had no doubt he would do it well
enough. To make her believe. To make her *imagine*.

To make her tell herself even more stories, then
believe them even though she knew better.

That ache inside her bloomed again, sharper
than before. Her head pounded.

But she had come to a stop on the stair, and that
was the part that seemed the most like an indict-
ment. Like shame.

"Come now, *mia mogliettina*," came the dark
voice she most and least wanted to hear, seeming to envelop her from above. "You do not truly
believe that I would allow this to happen again,
do you?"

She was so close to the bottom of the stairs,
but she'd stopped. Had she sensed him? Had she
known he was near?

Why did she want that to matter?

"Let me go, Ago," she said softly.

It was more as if she felt him move than actually heard it. The weight of him, as if gravity hung differently from a man hewn from steel and so many centuries. The force of him, so intense, so bold, and tonight, wrapped up in a dark fury.

She did not have to turn around to know he came down the stairs behind her. And when he spoke again, that he was closer only made the storm in him seem to rage through her, too.

"Surely you understand by now that I have no intention of ever letting you go, Victoria," he said, like he was handing down judgment and a sentence in one. "Did you imagine I would?"

She turned then, not at all surprised to find him only a couple of steps above her. Still, it was enough that she had to crane her head back to look at him, making her feel something like seasick.

And all the while the moon poured in through the windows, making love to him, wreathing him in all that silver.

He looked like some kind of pagan god, clad only in silk that rode dangerously low on his hips. The whole of his chest just gleamed there, impossibly beautiful, as if he was a Michelangelo piece, sculpted out of marble or dipped in bronze, made for no other purpose than to create awe in all who beheld him.

It worked.

But he had asked her a question, so she ignored that awestruck feeling inside. She ignored the bronze, the silvery light, the marble expanse of his perfectly formed chest—and the knowledge that if she moved closer, he would not be as cold as he might look in all this moonlight. He would be hot to the touch. The heat of him would soak into her, making her feel warm and alive, though even that was nothing next to his taste. His scent.

And she knew she would carry that with her, too.

"I want you to let me go because I'm asking you to," she told him softly, so softly that she hoped he couldn't hear the tightness in her throat. "And Ago. Please remember that I have never asked you for anything. Only this."

"Because you do not need to ask," he growled at her, his voice like thunder, rolling through her, warning her. Making everything in her seem to stand at attention. "Have I not provided everything you could possibly want? I make you cry out in joy, it is so intense. I clothe you. I import your childhood, so that you might feel easy here. I gave you Christmas. What else do you want?"

She found herself rubbing at the sides of her belly, as if that could somehow make the pain that was building inside again go away. "I don't want to be treated like a *pet*, Ago. Why can't you understand?"

But she knew even as she asked that he didn't understand. That he couldn't.

Maybe it was unfair to even ask such a thing of him. Then again, she remembered how she'd felt, standing there outside his office and listening to the things he said to her father. And *fairness* no longer felt like much of a priority.

"I don't expect you to understand," she told him, hardly recognizing her own voice, it sounded so…ragged. Something like torn. "After all, how could I expect you to treat me differently than you treat yourself? Tethered to this place. To this legacy of yours. To the things old men told you that you have taken as gospel, holding them to you so tightly you can't see past them."

"All I see is a woman who has been given everything, yet still wishes to shirk her responsibilities," he ground out.

"I never asked for these responsibilities."

"And you imagine I did?" he retorted. He shook his head. "I was unaware that responsibilities became a menu, to be chosen or not chosen as one pleases. I have never known such luxury. And I'm sorry to tell you this, *mia mogliettina*, but that is not a luxury available to you, either."

"Well, it bloody well should be," Victoria threw back at him. She was still holding her sides and now she was panting a little, though she couldn't have said if it was because of the temper that coursed through her, or whatever that pain was inside her now, that felt more and more like a deep throbbing thing.

She tried to make herself breathe through it.

He came down to her step and his face looked so hard, almost cruel in the moonlight. Yet when he reached out to wrap his hand around her upper arm his grip, though firm, was not painful. She knew he controlled himself even now.

For some reason, that did not please her at all.

"You and I do not get *shoulds*, Victoria," he seethed at her. "It seems to me that what you wish you had was a different life. Sadly, that is not a choice available to you. I'm sorry that your childhood was difficult. Whose wasn't? And some might claim that all of this is the wanderlust that you were not permitted under your father's thumb, but I don't think that's true. I think the truth is that you're trying to outrun the inevitable."

She forgot the pain inside her, the way her head ached, to scowl at him. "And that's you, I suppose? You consider yourself inevitable?"

"I am inescapable," he told her, his gaze a bright and glittering warning. "But what is inevitable is that you are about to become a mother. However you may feel about your childhood, it is over now. There is no going back. There is no undoing this. I think this scares you down to your marrow."

"While I think you're projecting," she threw right back at him, even though, in and around the discomfort she felt in her belly, something seemed to…quake.

"I don't need to project such things," he bit out at her. "I know exactly who I am, and that was never a child like some, left to amuse myself as I pleased. Unlike you, I do not mourn the loss of something I never had. Because I know its purpose."

His hand tightened, just slightly, on her upper arm, and something flared between them.

And all Victoria could think about was the word *love*. It seemed to expand inside of her, like some kind of inexorable balloon, filling up all the available space and crowding everything else out—

Yet all the more painful because she knew that wasn't the word he would choose.

It wasn't what he was going to say.

"The Accardi legacy," he intoned, because of course that's what he said. Because to him, that was the only thing that mattered. "And I have tried to make this easy for you, Victoria."

She managed to crack out a kind of laugh at that. "Have you? Funny, *easy* isn't the word I would have chosen."

He dropped his hand from her arm, but only so he could glare down at her as if his will alone could transform her into whatever shape he wished. And staring up at him, Victoria couldn't quite imagine how she'd ever seen anything in him but this unbending sternness. This ruthless disregard for anything but this, his favorite topic.

"But here you are, on Christmas, attempting to run off yet again," Ago said with a quiet intensity that seemed to jar her, deep inside. "You do not wish to be treated like a pet, so perhaps you should cease behaving like a recalcitrant one. But it doesn't matter. Because I am finished."

She felt wobbly, and tried to lecture herself. She needed to straighten her knees. She needed to stand tall and proud as she faced whatever terrible thing he was about to say to her. "Finished?"

Victoria knew that he did not mean divorce. That was not who he was. But somehow, that was not as comforting as it ought to have been.

"You may think that this has been difficult for you, but you haven't seen anything," he told her, his voice grimmer with every word. "I spent my entire childhood watching as my mother was kept medicated. Under lock and key, not even permitted to visit a bathroom on her own, in the bad years. Do you imagine I would do anything less if I deemed it necessary?"

"My understanding is that your mother was very ill," she managed to get out.

"Did she start that way or did she become that way?" Ago shook his head, his dark eyes flashing. "On some level, I thought my own father a monster for containing my mother here as he did, no matter how often he professed his love. But now I must assume he did what was required, no matter how unsavory. Because my mother knew nothing of a world like this. Of the things that the Accardi name asked of her."

Victoria could hardly breathe, but he wasn't finished.

"She wasn't like you, Victoria," Ago told her, as if he was already locking her away. "She was not specifically crafted for a life like this. I can find it within me to excuse my mother's failures. But yours?" He shook his head. "I will not tolerate this. I will chain you up if I have to. I will do anything and everything to protect the legacy I've given the whole of my life to. I will not play these games with you."

And everything around her seemed uneven, as if the stair she stood upon had become the sea, and wave after wave attempted to take her feet out from under her. But somehow, she managed to focus. On Ago, gleaming in the moonlight.

On Ago, who she loved despite herself.

"Your legacy," she managed to say. "It's really

the only thing you speak of, isn't it? And yet you keep missing the point."

"Wrong again," he growled at her.

"All of this is nothing," she told him. Her tongue felt fuzzy. But she stepped back, off that last step, so she could swing her arm wide to take in the villa, him, and all of Tuscany slumbering in the moonlight outside. "It's a house. It's *stuff.* And most of all it's stories that people told you, that you accepted whole. Uncritically. But at the end of the day, what can any of that matter?"

"At the end of the day," he said, with great deliberation, "it's the only thing that matters. And I will succeed in preserving it if it is the last thing I do."

"But that's the thing, Ago," she said, even as she could no longer tell the difference between the floor beneath her and the walls all around. Even though she could no longer seem to focus on him the way she knew she should. "You're going to fail. You already have. Because the only thing in this life that really matters is love, and you think it's a weakness."

Victoria wanted to say more. She wanted to tell him so many things. That she loved him anyway, against her own interests. That she thought she would have loved him even if there was no baby, and no reason for them to be thrown together like this. She wanted to tell him that she wished they could start over, way back a year ago, when Ago had come to her father's house for what she realized only in retrospect was an audition.

What would have happened if she'd followed that strange compulsion she'd had that night? If she'd ignored her father's posturing and told this man, no matter how forbidding he looked, that he was the only one of the many suitors her father had made her perform in front of that actually made her feel something?

She wanted to touch him, one last time, so she could carry it with her when she left.

But she didn't do any of those things.

Because everything inside her seemed to scrape to a terrible stop. A wave of something terrible shuddered through her.

And the last thing Victoria saw was a look of terrible alarm on Ago's face before everything went black.

CHAPTER TEN

AGO SAW THE color drain from her face, and was moving without thought, lunging across the very little space between them to catch Victoria in his arms as she toppled toward the floor.

And when he could not get her eyes to open, nor any response, he began to shout.

Like the world was ending.

Because that was how it felt.

Especially when his own harsh words echoed inside him.

It seemed to take lifetimes for his staff to respond. To catch up with him as he strode through the house and out into the courtyard, headed for the stables where the medical team was stationed.

Lifetimes with her lifeless form in his arms while inside, something beat at him, low and hard, shame and horror, because he knew this was his fault.

Why had he said such things to her? But he

knew. He had woken to find her creeping away from him, when he had made himself vulnerable before her with that nursery without even meaning to—

And hadn't his father told him directly that this would happen?

Had it been made clear that he would hurt her if he loved her?

He nearly staggered at the truth of that.

A truth he had not been able to face when he'd found her on the stairs, leaving him *yet again*—

The lights blazed on in the villa behind him and in the stables ahead of him. He barely felt the cold or noticed the dark outside until he was shouldering his way into the stables, shouting for the doctor and nurse. Only the heat inside made him realize it had been frigid out there.

But he didn't care, because Victoria wasn't conscious and that was impossible.

This was *impossible*.

The medical staff came running then.

And everything sped up again.

He was unaware of the hour, or how long things took. For every moment was an agony, both too quick and too long, and none of it mattered anyway, because Victoria did not wake up.

She did not wake and he had only himself to blame.

The medical team did what they could. But

when she was stabilized, Ago had her taken to the airfield on his property, loaded as carefully as possible on his plane, and then flew her to England.

Where, by morning, he had her under the care of the finest neonatal doctors in Britain.

What did he care if it was their Boxing Day?

They threw all kinds of alarming words at him. *Preeclampsia. Potential fetal distress.* And though he took it in, asked questions, and demanded that his staff research it all so that he became an expert as quickly as possible—none of that was *doing* anything.

Because there was nothing to do.

There was nothing at all for Ago Accardi, for whom mountains usually moved at a single soft command, but the endless waiting.

And nothing but self-flagellation to go with it.

It was unbearable.

For forty-eight hours, he did not move from her bedside. He maintained his vigil, as if the simple fact of his presence would make her wake up when the doctors assured him she *could.* That there was no medical reason for her to remain unconscious when they had stabilized her condition and made sure the baby was safe.

But she didn't.

And on the third day, Ago left the hospital because it was that or start physically accosting the doctors who did not seem to understand that he needed his wife to wake up, immediately. He took the hospital's private exit, because his staff had informed him that there were already too many paparazzi gathered at the usual entrance.

Because word had apparently got out that Ago Accardi had rushed into hospital, bearing a pregnant woman who was rumored to be his wife.

A woman who had once been *this close* to being engaged to his brother.

It was the very nightmare Ago had been hoping to avoid this whole time, and yet he found that he didn't care.

The only thing that mattered was Victoria waking up, and there was literally nothing he could do to make that happen. If the paparazzi and their dirty little tabloids could have helped her, he would have gone out and fed them anything and everything he wanted to hear.

And instead of sitting in his excruciatingly pedigreed house in Belgravia and driving himself up his elegantly appointed walls, Ago found himself driving out of London entirely.

Then heading for a part of England he had never visited. Because touring the idyllic Cotswolds, swooning over wisteria and pretty limestone cottages, had never appealed to a man who knew his primary purpose on this earth was to expand an empire. Not to enjoy weekends away like some kind of regular person. Perish the thought.

In fact, the closest thing he'd had to a holiday in as long as he could remember were these last weeks with Victoria. And it was true that he'd spent almost every day of them working in some capacity or another, but when he wasn't working, he hadn't been thinking about work at all. That was the difference.

When Victoria was around, the only thing he seemed to think about was her.

That notion—that he hadn't allowed himself to admit before—was still turning over and over inside him, like a virus, when he found his way to a tiny house on the outskirts of yet another near-supernaturally lovely village. He pulled up outside, staring balefully at the cozy little cottage that bore the correct address on the front door, set behind a picturesque stone wall with a gate. It had been snowing on his drive out and the tiny house was covered in just enough of the stuff to make it look fluffy. He could see curls of smoke coming from the chimney, and there were candles in every window, casting the kind of good cheer out into the morning that made him feel nothing so much as baleful.

Possibly even broken, when he had never permitted himself even a moment of such self-indulgence in his life. It was nice for some that they got to

waffle about, claiming brokenness and all manner of maladies, but *he* had always had work to do.

He sat there, gripping the steering wheel of
the SUV that had delivered him here. And he
thought the vehicle was emblematic of this life
that felt so suddenly meaningless all around him.
He didn't remember buying it. Probably because
he had nothing to do with its purchase. He could
tell that it was a newer model, quietly elegant and
yet capable.

It wasn't lost on him that he'd expected to view
his wife in much the same way.

He had considered Victoria a perfect wife in
theory, not least because she was so likely to be
useful and quietly competent, but their marriage
had never settled into that kind of functional ease.
Instead, there was this monstrous swamp of emotion inside of him.

It had been growing, day by day, since that ren-
dezvous in her uncle's garden.

And had only gotten worse after Rome.

What Ago had been unable to stop thinking of,
these last few days, was that he had been losing
himself in a woman for the first time in his life.
The only time.

And all the while, she had been intending to
leave him.

Again.

Shameful though it was, he had not been kidding when he told her he was perfectly prepared to take extraordinary measures to keep her with him.

He'd known every member of his staff since he was a boy. He knew they would obey him without question. If he truly wished to chain his new wife to their bed, they would have happily obliged him.

Ago knew that he would have had no qualm whatsoever, and surely that should have scared him more than it did.

Not that it mattered, for now the only thing he wanted was for her to wake up.

So he could tell her that the world only made sense with her in it and he no longer cared where in that world she needed to locate herself.

He didn't care what freedom looked like for her. So long as she was alive and well and happy.

Ago was almost certain he meant that.

There was a pounding at his window and he blinked, having completely forgotten where he was.

Outside, Tiziano stood beside the SUV, looking in at Ago with a quizzical sort of smile on his face.

"Are you coming in, brother?" he asked through the glass. "I rather thought you were the paparazzi."

Ago pushed open the door and stepped out, not even wincing as the cold rushed at him. In truth, he hardly felt it.

"It's not like you to drop by without an itemized

itinerary," Tiziano was saying, looking entirely too pleased with himself. *Smug*, Ago thought— or, then again, perhaps he was just jealous that his younger brother had found a way to give himself over entirely to emotion, and seemed to be the better for it. "An itinerary, a month's notice, an advance team to scout out the area—"

"Victoria collapsed," Ago belted out, out there in the crisp Gloucestershire morning. And once he'd said it, he couldn't stop. "The baby is fine, though it was touch and go there for a moment. But she won't wake up." He found himself scowling at his brother, or maybe that was not the right way to describe the thing that was happening to him. That was taking over his face. "She *won't wake up*, Tiziano."

He regretted saying anything the moment the words were out. He didn't even know why he was here. He had spent the whole of his life trying to whip his brother into shape. Trying to mold Tiziano into proper shape and form, according to all the rules he'd lived by his whole life. And Tiziano had disappointed him, every time.

Yet he'd gotten into the car and driven here with no real idea what he was doing.

"I don't know why I've rousted you out of your little love nest into all this snow," he gritted out. "I should have rung."

But there was an expression he'd never seen before on his younger brother's face. Tiziano reached out and clapped him on the shoulder. Then, astonishingly, slung his arm over Ago.

"Don't be silly," he said, but there was no trace of his trademark laughter in his voice. If Ago wasn't mistaken, it was all compassion. He wasn't sure how he felt about that, but then, he wasn't sure how he felt about anything. "You'd better come in."

Ago thought that really, he'd better get back to the hospital, but it seemed his body had other ideas. Because before he knew it, Tiziano was leading him inside. And it was the tiniest house Ago had ever seen. He had to duck to make it past the lintel, and he thought that if he dared pull in a deeper breath, he might smack his head on the ceiling. But inside, there was music playing, and everything smelled of Christmas trees and sugar. His brother's woman—who Ago understood, today, was going to become his brother's wife—peered out of what was clearly a kitchen, passed some silent communication with Tiziano, and then disappeared with only a little wave Ago's way.

But Ago didn't know what he was supposed to do now that he was…here. Inside this cottage. This…*love nest*. He went and sat, gingerly, on one of the tiny couches. His brother stood by the fireplace, looking somehow both languid and intent at once.

"I'll start," Tiziano said when the silence between them had dragged down so long that Ago thought he could likely sing the entirety of "I'll Be Home For Christmas," when he had gone to such lengths to avoid paying attention to all the mawkishly sentimental carols until now. "You seem to be in quite a state about Victoria Cameron, Ago. She is quite beautiful, I grant you, but I thought that the major point in her favor was the ease with which she would fade into any given background. Her main talent, if you will. Because, truly, Everard Cameron is a tedious man. It's only reasonable that his only daughter should also be a great bore."

"You don't know her."

Ago didn't recall shooting to his feet, but there he was, standing up and risking decapitation with every breath. It took him longer than it should to realize that his brother was smiling.

"Do I not?" Tiziano asked mildly. "Perhaps you had better tell me about her, then."

"She's maddening," Ago belted out. "Headstrong. Ungrateful. Absolutely reckless. Do know what she was doing when she collapsed? Leaving me. *Me*. And not for the first time. The first time, she was gallivanting all across Italy, eating gelato and disregarding both my instructions and her duty."

"Shocking behavior," murmured Tiziano. "*Gelato*, I ask you. What's next? Will she storm the papal residence?"

"I'm sure you find this hilarious," Ago bit out, because it was very near a pleasure to have a focus for all this *mess* in him. And what better target was there than a brother as annoying as his? "This is what you have always wanted, is it not? Well, I congratulate you. I am saddled with a scandalous, wholly inappropriate wife when you know full well I cannot afford such a thing."

Tiziano shrugged. "Then divorce her."

Ago had been angry with his brother before. Incandescently so, in fact, and more than once.

But he had never, in all his life, wanted to take Tiziano apart limb by limb. With his own hands.

And that was just a start.

Somehow, he remembered himself. Somehow, he pulled himself from the brink. "Don't be absurd. Divorce is not an option."

Another indolent shrug. "Why not?"

Ago scowled at him. "Have you taken leave of your senses? You know as well as I do that Accardis do not divorce."

"My mistake," his brother said, sounding suspiciously casual. "Because it is far preferable to be endlessly unhappy and raise your children so that they will be miserable too, all to preserve…what? Some notion of a legacy?" Tiziano's gaze, uncomfortably too like Ago's own, seemed to pierce him where he stood. "I have a radical idea, brother. What if you figured out how to be happy? Imagine if that were your legacy."

That was disturbingly close to what Victoria had said, that Ago wished he could get out of his head. Just as he wished that he could banish, forever, the sight of her going over all pale, her eyes rolling back in her head, and coming so close to cracking her head open right there on his stairwell.

At his feet.

He felt as if the floor of this rickety old cottage was rocking and buckling beneath him, though he knew it wasn't.

He hated it.

But he still knew who he was. Maybe that was all he had left. "I know that you have rejected this your whole life, but it was beaten into me from a young age. What matters is duty. Dedication to our history, our future. All of this sits upon my shoulders, Tiziano." He shook his head. "The Accardi legacy isn't simply my guiding light, it's who I am."

"But what if," his brother said, inexorably, "you were someone else instead?"

And if, at any other time, Tiziano had said such

a thing to him, Ago would have brushed it off. It was Tiziano playing his usual games, he would have thought. It was Tiziano and his usual inability to grasp the realities of things. Because he was the younger son and it had been different for him. He could do as he liked. He'd enjoyed a freedom that Ago never had, and never would.

And maybe it was that he thought that word. *Freedom.*

Such a simple thing, or so Victoria seemed to think. Was it possible that the reason he had never thought much of it was because he'd never known it himself?

Did it matter how big a cage was? Or was the point of a cage that the occupant couldn't leave?

Ago didn't know. What he did know was that, for once, he stared back at his brother and didn't dismiss him out of hand.

And something shifted in Tiziano's expression. He blinked, then straightened from the fire.

"You used to be someone else, Ago," Tiziano said quietly. "I doubt you even remember. But before you were the worthy scion, you were a little boy. You were funny. You laughed. You made a ruckus. You took great pleasure in pulling pranks, playing games. And when the nannies could persuade you to sit still, you amused yourself by drawing caricatures that made even Father laugh." He laughed, but it wasn't his usual, notorious laughter. This sounded far more bleak. "Of all the things I would hold our parents accountable for, if they lived, I think that might top the list. They drained the life out of that boy. And ruined him."

"It's called growing up."

But Ago's voice was rough. And he felt that roughness straight through.

"Does she love you?" Tiziano asked.

And something inside of Ago seem to shake, and keep shaking, until it broke. It was a shattering so intense that he wasn't sure that there would be anything left of him at all when it was done.

If it was ever done, for there seemed to be no end in sight.

"How would I know?" he gritted out.

And though inside him everything was shattered glass and a deep howling, he could still see the way his brother's face filled with the sort of compassion he would have said Tiziano did not possess. When really, now that he was seeing things more clearly than perhaps he ever had before, he suspected that he was the one lacking these crucial building blocks that everyone else on earth seem to possess.

Especially Victoria.

He thought of the way she'd melted in his arms. He thought of the way she'd given herself over to him when they had come back from Rome, holding nothing back. He had a simple, perfect memory that could have been from any morning at all. Catching up with her as she walked through the fields and tangling his fingers with hers. The passion between them might have kept them up at night, but it was the simple things that he remembered now. The way she had always held on so tight. The way she tipped her head up to look at him, and smiled.

He could not recall ever deserving her generosity, but she had given it anyway.

He remembered their evenings together, lingering at the table as they had debated the kinds of things he hadn't spoken about with anyone since his Cambridge days. The merit of this novel or that. Some bit of philosophy, or scrap of poetry she'd read. He had been shocked to discover that Victoria, while unable to boast of the sort of Oxbridge education he'd had as a matter of course, had read widely, deeply, and with the kind of rapt attention he wasn't sure that most Cambridge first years gave to their subject matter.

Not even him.

When he'd said something to that effect, she had made a face.

What else was there to do in all my years of genteel imprisonment? She had laughed at that, though now, Ago wasn't sure that he would. *The entire purpose of books is to expand even the most limited horizons. I know they did mine.*

And there he'd been, with every advantage of the world and more besides, thundering about threatening to limit her even further. While she stood at the base of the stairs, surrounded by portraits of his ancestors, ripe and round with his child.

And she'd spoken to him of love, the one thing he knew nothing about.

"Our father loved our mother," he said now, though it hurt him. And he thought it hurt his brother to hear it, too. "Do you remember that he always said so? With all his heart, he loved her. And in the end, it was her undoing."

Tiziano stared. And then, slowly, ran a hand over his face. "I suppose it could have been a factor," he said, not quite committing to his usual drawl. "But I rather think it had more to do with the opiates."

Ago couldn't process that. His heart set up a wild clamor behind his ribs. "What? You are mistaken. She was unwell."

"She was an addict," Tiziano corrected him, and not as if he had the slightest doubt. "And more than that, brother, she was a selfish woman who was remarkably good at blaming everyone around her for her problems."

"I have no idea what you're talking about."

Tiziano's mouth curved, though his eyes were bleak. "Of course you don't. It was kept from you, the better to hammer into you that you and you alone should stand as the paragon of virtue they never were. Grandfather was eternally outraged that he was unable to convince our grandmother that she ought to love him when she'd made it clear she never would. And Father? Where do you think a simple girl like our mother learned to experiment with so many lovely pills? Neither one of them ever stopped to consider that the main problem in their marriages was them."

Ago couldn't tell, now, if the floor beneath him was moving or the world was suddenly spinning too fast. He only knew he was near enough to dizzy with it, and he couldn't seem to tear his gaze away from his brother.

While Tiziano said these things that should have been impossible.

Even if some of what he said Ago already knew was true, because Victoria had told him.

"What you're saying is not possible," Ago argued anyway, with the strange, unsteady notion deep inside that he was fighting for his life. "They were the best of men. Upright, dutiful, wholly dedicated—"

"To rolling responsibility downhill, Ago," Tiziano cut in. And he was warming to the subject. "To pretending that any problem they had was yours to solve. Talking endlessly about legacies, and doing nothing to preserve their own."

Ago could only stare at his brother, though he was afraid that all he could see were the ghosts of the men he'd spent his life trying to make proud of him.

In a way, he had seen nothing but them, all this time.

And Tiziano was still speaking. "And even if you don't believe a word I'm saying, think of this. Both of them died bitter men. Is that what you want? Both of their wives preferred the company of intoxicants to their presence. Does that sound appealing to you? Think, Ago. You have a child on the way."

"Son," Ago managed to croak out. "Victoria is giving me a son."

Tiziano moved then, stepping toward Ago as if he couldn't stop himself. As if he didn't try.

"Ago," he gritted out. "Brother. Be honest for the first time in your life. I beg of you."

Ago wanted to argue that he was nothing but honest. That he'd spent his life being excruciatingly honest, and that had cost him.

But he found that standing here in this enchanted cottage, drowning in all the rest of these things he could not understand—or perhaps understood too well, as little as he liked it—he couldn't seem to say a word.

His younger brother looked at him and saw all of him. Ago could see that he did. Not just who Ago had become, but that mischievous little boy that Ago himself hardly remembered. Bright. Fearless. Funny.

Not irresponsible, but not eaten alive with a sense of duty. Not any more reckless than any other child while, at the same time, not unaware that big things would be expected of him one day.

Then his grandfather had started to get sick. And his father had gotten angrier. Ago supposed his mother was a factor too, though he had never been encouraged to examine that situation. Not the way Tiziano clearly had.

And the very thought of treating the child Victoria carried the way he had been treated...

It made him want to break things.

And Tiziano, damn him, saw that, too.

"Do you really want to do to your son what was done to you?" he asked quietly, but the words seemed to land inside Ago like stones. One after the next. "What would happen if you just loved him, Ago? The way they should have loved us. The way they couldn't."

"Tiziano," Ago began. He shook his head. "I have underestimated you."

His brother grinned. "I have wanted you to," he replied. "I prefer it that way."

Then he reached out and gripped Ago's shoulder, with a fire blazing in his dark blue gaze that took no quarter. "Ask yourself what would happen, Ago. What if you took your wife and your son as an opportunity to make your own legacy, once and for all?"

CHAPTER ELEVEN

VICTORIA WOKE, CONFUSED.

There was someone leaning over her and she understood at once that she was in hospital, for there was the beeping and there was something stuck in her hand—

And the next second she knew nothing but sheer panic.

"My baby," she managed to croak out, though her voice felt treacherous in her throat, and came out like a stranger's. *"Is my baby all right?"*

The nurse above her made soothing noises. "Settle down, Mrs. Accardi," she said. In an accent that told Victoria that she was not in Italy any longer. "Your baby is fine. You are fine. You've just given us a scare, that's all."

But Victoria was already struggling to sit up. She was pressing her hands all over her belly, finding the baby's head, but feeling nothing—and not believing for even one second that she would be in a hospital if something terrible hadn't happened.

Then in the next moment, the baby kicked, punishingly. Then again, as if he thought it was a fine time to trampoline against her diaphragm.

It was wildly uncomfortable, even as she hissed in a breath. And still, the joy was so intense that she didn't care how it was she'd come to be here or what else might be wrong. As long as it was wrong with her, not him. She wiped at her face with the hand that wasn't connected to all these machines, not caring at all that it was trembling.

And that was when she saw him.

Belatedly, the fact that the nurse had called her *Mrs. Accardi* sunk in. It was the right thing to call her, of course, but she hadn't heard anyone say that in the whole of her short-lived marriage.

But there was no time to think about that, because looking at Ago made the rest come rushing back.

That oddly perfect Christmas, even though she knew she planned to leave. The nursery, and what it meant that he'd gone to such trouble for no other reason than to make her happy. How desperately she'd wanted to believe that something like that meant more than it did.

Because there she'd been, falling in love. While he'd been prettying up the cage.

Although she had to admit, looking at him now, that it was hard not to wonder if she might have overreacted.

Ago looked…rough, for him. He was not clean-shaven. The stubble on his jaw lent him a roguish sort of air that seemed to make everything inside and out prickle. He was wearing trousers and a fine cashmere jumper that she understood was casual, for him. There was no suit in sight.

He looked like he'd been awake for days. She wanted to go to him and put her hand on his face, to assure herself that he was okay. Even if she was maybe not okay herself.

Victoria was sitting in a hospital bed, suffering from God knew what, and still. When his dark blue gaze found hers and held, her whole body tightened and between her legs, she felt a rush of that same delirious heat.

In case she wondered if thinking she was in love with him had been a temporary madness in the villa.

"I don't remember what happened," she said softly. "I was on the stairs…?"

"Thank you," Ago said to the nurse, taking command of the room with his usual swiftness. "That will be all for now."

The nurse was nodding as he spoke. "I'll let the doctor know that Mrs. Accardi is awake."

She hustled out, closing the door behind her, and Ago took his time looking back at Victoria. He stayed where he was, standing there against the far wall, and she knew, somehow. That he'd been here. However many hours or days, he'd been here. With her.

Right there in that chair he stood beside.

"The press are already trying to batter down the doors outside," he said, but not in that dark way she would have expected. It seemed at odds with how rugged and rough he looked. "No need to give them more fodder, I think. I much prefer the stories they make up, if I'm honest. They are always far more entertaining."

Victoria blinked. "Did I hit my head? Is that what this is? Am I in a coma, dreaming that Ago Accardi would make light of the fact that the paparazzi are onto him?" It took her a moment to think about what that must mean. "Does that mean they know about me?"

"Oh yes," Ago said, and though there was something she didn't recognize in his voice, it wasn't the grim censure she would have expected. "It's been quite a palaver, these last few days. While you have been napping, Victoria, every tabloid in Europe has been competing to tell the most lurid version of how and when we met, whether you ever intended to marry my brother, and who, indeed, is the father of your baby. If I'm honest, I think they've all missed Tiziano's former indiscretions. They've taken to this one with sheer delight."

Too many questions flooded her head, and Victoria shook it without thinking. Then she froze, waiting to feel some kind of pain. She had a fleeting memory of that awful headache—

But there was nothing. She didn't feel quite like herself, perhaps. But there was no pain. Not even those cramps she vaguely remembered from Christmas night.

"Ago," she said quietly. "I don't understand what's going on. Why am I here? What happened? Are we absolutely, one hundred percent certain that the baby is all right?"

"I have asked that very question myself," he told her, with the great seriousness she expected of him. It was comforting. "Of every prenatal specialist in this hospital and all of the United Kingdom. And as far as anyone can tell, the baby is fine. It's you who had them concerned."

She was aghast. "I didn't hurt him, did I?"

"No, *mia mogliettina*, you did not hurt him." Ago's voice was something like soft, and that confused her. "But he came very close to hurting you."

"That's fine," she said, frowning down at her bump, and rubbing the hard jut of her baby's head in sheer relief. Such relief she could feel herself begin to tear up. "I can make it another couple of months or so."

"About that."

She looked up again to find him moving toward

her, coming to sit in the chair beside her bed. And then he stunned her by reaching over and taking her hand in his.

"You have only ever asked me for one thing, Victoria. Do you remember?"

Victoria felt her lips part, and inside, the strangest wave of emotion move through her. Though still, the last thing she could remember was walking down the stairs in the villa. And then knowing that he was behind her, as inevitable as the coming of the dawn.

"I asked you for something?" She tried to smile in her usual serene way, but found she couldn't. "That doesn't sound like me."

"You should have no qualm in the world ever asking me for anything," he told her then, with a sudden flash of passion. The sort of passion she would anticipate hearing only when he was deep inside her. But he wasn't. "You should not only ask for anything and everything, Victoria. You should expect that your husband will do whatever is necessary to give you anything you ask, and more. That is the very least of what you should expect from me."

Her heart leapt wildly in her chest, and once again, she felt as if there was some kind of hand at her throat. But this time, she couldn't tell if she wanted to break this tension between them, or lean into it.

But it didn't matter, because he was still talking. "You asked me for your freedom, and you shall have it."

"Oh," Victoria said, with her hand in his. Lost somewhere in that deep blue gaze of his. *Freedom* was the last thing on her mind. "Um. Thank you?"

He held her hand tighter, but she liked that. "I only ask one thing. The doctors have said that they would be happier if you remained on bed rest for the remainder of your pregnancy. I am hoping you will allow me to make this as easy on you as possible. Only until the baby is born." Ago's throat moved and she understood that this was hard for him. "After that, you may do as you please. With my blessing."

Victoria was certain that she was dreaming now. Then again, his hand held hers and she could feel his heat. His strength. She could see the intensity on his face. And besides that, there was the bright sheen of honesty in his gaze.

It was her undoing.

But she remembered now. She remembered hearing him on the phone with her father and her sickening realization that it was all a lie. "I suppose this is just another version of what you do, isn't it?" she asked, and she felt as if she was screaming even though she knew she wasn't. "Using our child as ransom. Using whatever you can to make me do what you want. I tried to tell you, Ago. I've already done this." She shook her head. "Surely there has to be a better legacy than this."

She expected him to drop her hand. To pull back, draw himself up to his impressive height, and thunder at her the way he did. Maybe she was remembering it or maybe she simply knew him, but either way, she braced herself for him to take her apart. To point out all the ways she was deficient and should be grateful that he bothered with her.

Had he threatened to *chain* her?

But Ago didn't move.

"I agree with you." He lifted her hand and pressed a kiss to her knuckles, though his gaze remained trained to hers. "How about love?"

And it was as if everything just…stopped.

Victoria was surprised that she could still hear the beeping of the machines she was connected to.

She realized she didn't believe her ears. "What?"

"If love is the only legacy that matters, *mia mogliettina*, then love is the only legacy I will dedicate myself to," he told her. And when she stared at him blankly, his mouth curved. "That is what you told me, *mia amata. Cuore mio.* Before you fell into my arms and I thought you were dead."

Victoria gazed back at him, her lips parting as she tried to take in what was happening.

And at the same time, tried to remind herself that this was likely all an act…even if she felt, deep in her bones, that it was nothing of the sort.

As if he could read all of that on her face, Ago's expression turned solemn, though his eyes still burned. "I want to promise you, here and now, that all the vows we took in that chapel mean something. I want to love you, honor you. I want to care for you and our child, and never do to him what was done to me. I would promise you all of these things right now, and I would want to mean them with all my soul, but the simple truth is that I have never done them." He shook his head. "I was taught from a young age that love was the enemy. And I suspect that I will not be any good at it. But for you, *mia adorabile mogliettina*, I will try. Every day, every hour, I will try."

And she knew better. She knew that there was nothing in this life more dangerous than hope— though try she might, she couldn't seem to keep it at bay. It flooded into her, kicking all around, knocking down walls and making her think…

What if?

And she had the strangest notion that all the freedom she could ever dream of was waiting for her, right here, if she was just brave enough to make that leap.

Not away from him, but toward him.

Because there wasn't a single part of her that

wanted to leave him. No matter how she thought she *should.*

Victoria reached over with her other hand, so she could hold both of his. "It's all right," she told him softly. "I don't mind that you're inexperienced. Someone told me once that it's the enthusiasm that counts."

She watched as a kind of dawn broke over his dark face. Because he was the one who'd said that to her, long ago in her uncle's garden.

And just as he'd done then, Victoria smiled and leaned in a little closer. "Trust me."

"I love you," he said, and paused, as if tasting those words in his mouth. "I love you, Victoria. And I think, if I'm honest, I loved you the moment I saw you at that dinner in your father's house. But I couldn't make sense of it. It was unintelligible to me. I assumed the fact that I felt unsettled in your presence meant that I should disqualify you from any kind of consideration. I kept you close only way he knew how."

"By trying to fob me off on your brother," she said dryly. "It's practically a love poem."

But then, finally, she thought that this might be real after all. Because stern, uncompromising, relentlessly grim Ago lifted his hand so he could press a kiss to her knuckles again. One set, then the next.

And when he looked up at her again, he smiled.

In all that dark blue, she saw a gleaming light.

"I betrayed myself entirely for the chance to touch you in that garden," he told her, his voice rough and beautiful and laced through with something she'd never heard in him before. She thought it sounded a lot like joy. "And I would do it again. I did. You left me, and I hunted you down, and then had the brilliant idea that I would keep you with me by using sex. So certain was I that I could love you like that and feel nothing in return. But it didn't work. My only love, my heart, none of this has ever worked."

"Ago," she whispered, and even now, she couldn't get over the taste of his name in her mouth. "I would have married your brother, and happily, because it would have been easy. Friendly. Likely uncomplicated."

"I suspect there would have been complications," Ago murmured, shaking his head.

She smiled, brighter and happier than she could ever remember being before. "You and I might not be easy. On some days we might not even be friendly. But there will be joy. Sometimes it will be messy, because how could it not be, to love someone else like this? But it will be love. Because I loved you first. And I will love you forever. I can't wait for the rest of our lives, so I can show you."

"All you have to do is ask, my love," he said,

shifting so he could come closer yet, pressing his lips to her forehead, her cheeks, her lips. "Ask for anything at all, *mia mogliettina*, my forever love, and it is yours."

"But there's only one thing I want," she said, there against his mouth, scarcely daring to hope, scarcely daring to believe.

"Name it," he urged her.

And so she did. She tipped back her head and she lifted her hand to hold his face. His beloved, beautiful face.

"You," she whispered. "I want you, Ago. Only and ever you."

"But don't you see?" he murmured. "I have always been yours. Since the moment we met. And every moment after."

And only the fact that they were in a hospital room that anyone could enter at any time kept them from offering each other some proof, then and there.

CHAPTER TWELVE

A FEW DAYS LATER, Victoria celebrated the New Year wrapped up in her love in the villa, where Ago read her the tabloid reports of their scandalous relationship, and they laughed together. As if they were nothing more than fairy tales.

"Just a story, *mia amore*," Ago said one day when Victoria was cross about how they were being talked about in certain papers. "Remember, we know the real story."

The truth was, the real story was better. In every respect.

And it was theirs.

After giving them such a scare, their son entered the world late and loud. Cristiano Domenico Accardi was a menace from his very first breath.

They were smitten.

But that was when the true work began.

Things were not always easy. Neither one of them, when it came down to it, knew much of anything about love. Or the kind of healthy relationships it seemed some people knew how to have.

"Perhaps you can write in your diary for future generations," he growled at her after one unfortunate evening. "'Abandon hope, all ye who enter here.'"

"That would be quitting," she retorted.

And when Ago took exception to that, they worked out the way they always did. With a whole lot of talking—after a whole lot of expressing their differences in bed.

He told her, with great ceremony, that she ought to travel the world she saw fit, reveling in her freedom. But the truth was, the world that Victoria wanted to see was the world she saw with Ago. And so they traveled together, spending the first year of Cristiano's life going to every single place Victoria had been forbidden to explore on her own.

And even though they'd agreed that the next baby would be planned well in advance, nature had other ideas.

And so their second son, the deceptively cheerful Fabiano, was born only fifteen months after his older brother.

"I should tell you," said Ago the second morning of little Fabiano's life, as the baby suckled at her breast and Cristiano lay curled up at her side, his perfect cheeks flushed as he slept. "I have an enduring fantasy of you, ripe with our babies, again and again and again."

And Victoria knew it wasn't simply the rush of hormones, or the wild, mad love she felt for both of the little boys who clung to her then. She knew it wasn't even the way Ago looked at her from where he lay, propped up on one arm at the foot of their bed, gazing upon her as if he had never beheld anything so beautiful in all his life.

Maybe it was all of those things. But beyond that, it was simply…right.

It was right. It was them.

It was their story to tell as they wished.

She smiled at him as if her heart might break from all of this love. "I am an Accardi wife," she murmured. "It is my duty and my joy to obey."

And the legacy they left was one of laughter, and tears. More joy than pain. Seven pairs of little feet, charging in and around that villa. The ancient pile and surrounding countryside had more than enough breathing room for six wild Accardi sons, and one Accardi daughter, the ferocious Luna, who was named for the moon and terrorized them all.

Each time she was pregnant, her husband would draw her, then paint her, and his portraits graced the walls, in and around all those dour Accardi ancestresses. With their pain and their isolation, their angry diaries, their broken hearts.

Meanwhile the current matriarch was overflowing with love and life, round and ripe and, best of all, happy.

As she had suspected they could be the moment they'd met in London, she and her sister-in-law Annie became fast friends. And over the years, Tiziano and Annie's dangerously charming, gray-eyed children became more friends than cousins to Ago and Victoria's blue-eyed brood.

Making the kind of family Victoria had read about, but had never believed she would have.

And because she was a woman, not a saint, she invited her father to visit as often as possible. Because Everard could not abide the noise, or the way she raised her children as—in his view—wild animals.

"I think he thinks he's insulting me," she told Ago after one such visit.

"Let him," her husband murmured, his mouth at her neck.

Because the new baby was sleeping. And their need for each only grew. It only seemed to get brighter and hotter with age.

As if together, they created the perfect, dancing flame from all those sparks that had once marked them, and all those storms they'd learned how to dance in, together.

And for the rest of their days, they let it burn, and made sure that that was what they passed down to the children.

Not duty. Not sacrifice. But love, first and foremost.

Because nothing else mattered, unless there was love.

And in their house, there was so much love it made the walls shake a little. Loud and unruly, passionate and true.

So true that sometimes—only sometimes— her glorious husband let go of all his hard-won self-control and was as delightfully human as the rest of them.

Though only ever for her.

Just the way Victoria liked it.

* * * * *

#4073 INNOCENT MAID FOR THE GREEK
by Sharon Kendrick

Self-made Theo watched his new wife, Mia, flee minutes after signing their marriage papers. Now Theo must persuade the hotel maid to pretend to reunite for the sake of her grandfather's health. But being so close to her again is sensual torture!

#4074 PREGNANT IN THE ITALIAN'S PALAZZO
The Greeks' Race to the Altar
by Amanda Cinelli

Weeks after their passionate encounter on his private jet, Nysio can't get fashion designer Aria out of his head. He's determined to finish what they started! Only, in his palazzo, they discover something truly life-changing—she's expecting his baby!

#4075 REVEALING HER BEST KEPT SECRET
by Heidi Rice

When writer Lacey is told to interview CEO Brandon, she can't believe he doesn't recognize her—at all...even if her life has dramatically changed since their night together. Then their past and present collide and Lacey must reveal her biggest secret: their child!

#4076 MARRIAGE BARGAIN WITH HER BRAZILIAN BOSS
Billion-Dollar Fairy Tales
by Tara Pammi

After admitting her forbidden feelings for her boss, Caio, coding genius Anushka is mortified! So when he proposes they marry to save their business, she's conflicted. Because surely his ring, even his scorching touch, can never be enough without his heart...

#4077 A VOW TO SET THE VIRGIN FREE
by Millie Adams

Innocent Athena has escaped years of imprisonment...only to find herself captive in Cameron's Scottish castle! His marriage demand is unexpected but tempting. Because being bound to Cameron could give Athena more freedom than she believed possible...

#4078 CINDERELLA HIRED FOR HIS REVENGE
by Emmy Grayson

Grant longs to exact vengeance on the woman who broke his heart. When Alexandra needs his signature on a business-saving contract, he finally gets his opportunity. This time, when their passion becomes irresistible, *Grant* will be the one in control!

#4079 FORBIDDEN UNTIL THEIR SNOWBOUND NIGHT
Weddings Worth Billions
by Melanie Milburne

Aerin needs cynical playboy Drake to accompany her to a glamorous event in Scotland. She knows her brother's best friend *isn't* Mr. Right. But when a snowstorm leaves them stranded, she can't ignore the way Drake sets her pulse racing...

#4080 THE PRINCE'S ROYAL WEDDING DEMAND
by Lorraine Hall

The day innocent Ilaria stood in for her cousin on a date, she didn't expect it to be at the royal altar! And when Prince Frediano realizes his mistake, he insists Ilaria play her part of princess to perfection...

HPCNMRB1222

HARLEQUIN
PLUS

Announcing a **BRAND-NEW** multimedia subscription service for romance fans like you!

Read, Watch and Play.

Experience the easiest way to get the romance content you crave.

Start your **FREE 7 DAY TRIAL** at www.harlequinplus.com/freetrial.